BY CAROL MATAS

ALADDIN PAPERBACKS

NEW YORK LONDON TORONTO SYDNEY SINGAPORE

For Justin and Christa Brask,
with love.

This book is a work of fiction. Any references to historical events, real people, or real locales are used fictitiously. Other names, characters, places, and incidents are the product of the author's imagination, and any resemblance to actual events or locales or persons, living or dead, is entirely coincidental.

First Aladdin Paperbacks edition June 2003

Copyright © 2003 by Carol Matas

ALADDIN PAPERBACKS
An imprint of Simon & Schuster
Children's Publishing Division
1230 Avenue of the Americas
New York, NY 10020

Designed by Sammy Yuen Jr.
The text of this book was set in Utopia.

Printed in the United States of America
2 4 6 8 10 9 7 5 3 1

Library of Congress Control Number 2002013149

ISBN 0-689-85714-4

ACKNOWLEDGEMENTS:

I would like to thank the Lower East Side Tenement Museum and, in particular, Robin Marcato. It is a wonderful museum, and for anyone interested in life on the Lower East Side, make sure you visit. It also has an excellent Web site: http://www.tenement.org/.

I'd also like to thank my friend Perry Nodelman, who helped me break through to my story; my husband, Per Brask, who listened to the book chapter by chapter; and my editor, Jennifer Weiss, who was always supportive as well as insightful.

Chapter 1

"ROSIE!"

"What?"

"Here comes a swell!"

I could see him. A fancy man wearing a top hat was weaving his way through the crowded street.

My brother Abe and I held on to one end of a string. Across the street holding the other end of the string was my best friend, Maria, and Abe's friend Morris. I could see the swell's hat over the masses of caps and bonnets and as it hit the string it flew right off his head! He turned around and around, completely mystified. Abe pulled in the string, and, laughing, we dodged around the pushcart we'd been hiding behind.

"Come on," I said to Abe. "We're to meet in front of Mrs. Correlli's for the big game."

As we launched ourselves into the bustle of the

street, Mr. Roshevsky, who was selling bananas from a pushcart, called to us, "Don't you *dumkoppen* have anything better to do?"

Mr. Roshevsky had to be the crankiest person in the entire universe. Abe stuck his tongue out at him and kept going. But as usual, I answered back. "We don't," I said, unable to hide a small grin. "If we did, we'd be doing it, wouldn't we, Mr. Roshevsky?"

"Such a wise apple, you are," he said, shaking his head. "Here, take this. It won't sell and my day's almost over."

He handed me a banana that was mostly black, but I didn't care. I'd eat anything.

"Thanks, Mr. Roshevsky," I said, peeling and eating it as I spoke. "And by the way, I think you mean wise *aleck*."

"See?" he exclaimed. "That's just what I mean!"

"Come on!" Abe called.

I tried to catch up to him, but it was never easy to hurry on Orchard Street. The street was packed so tightly with pushcarts they took up every bit of curb. Men and women selling everything from buttons and stockings to chickens were yelling at the top of their lungs from behind the pushcarts: "Fresh apples! Just picked off the tree." "Look at this hat!

Only the finest!" "Scarves! All the colors of the rain-bow." "Fish! Fish so fresh, they're still breathing!" Right in front of me was a cart filled with plump oranges. It seemed I was always hungry no matter how much I ate. Mama says it's because I'm still growing. *Vaysmere!* I'm already a head taller than anyone else my age!

Abe grabbed me by the hand. He had come back for me.

"Rosie, stop drooling over the food! You'd think Mama didn't feed you."

"What a *nudzh* you are," I retorted. "Worse than Mama." Two years younger than me, yet he led me by the hand half the time, lecturing me while he was at it!

It was true that there was no time for dawdling. We had a very important game of ring-a-levio to play. I was to lead one team, Morris the other. We had at least ten people to a team. I allowed Abe to pull me along through the crowds to Mrs. Correlli's, and as I did so I began to put my mind to the game. Morris was younger than me, but he was smart. I needed a plan.

Of course, the most important thing was choosing my team. If I was clever in choosing, half the battle would be won. Last Sunday the game went on all day. If I chose well, maybe we could set a record and hold out two days, even three. If we won the toss, of course. If we didn't, we'd want to end the game as quickly as we could.

Abe and I had to squeeze in between Mr. Cohen's pretzel cart and Mrs. Karlinsky's pushcart full of shirts. I tried to ignore the heavenly smell coming from Mr. Cohen's cart. If it had been summer, we would have bought a penny's worth of ice cream from the hokeypokey man, but he stopped coming around weeks ago. Now the wind was sharp, and we were all hoping for snow.

"Never mind pretzels," Abe reminded me. "You have our fate in your hands."

"I know," I said. "I'm aware of the magnitude of my responsibility!"

Abe rolled his eyes. Whenever he nagged me, I tried to answer back with words so big, they would shut him up. Sometimes it worked.

By the time we reached Mrs. Corelli's, most of the players were already there. I scanned the faces deciding whom I'd choose first. I knew Maria would want me to choose her first, but that might not be smart, as she was a terrible player. True, she'd be upset, but winning was more important than that. Naturally, I wouldn't choose her last. That would be *too* cruel. Isaac had to be my number one pick. He lived in Mrs. Correlli's house. And he was the best player. Ruthless. Clever. Strong.

Maria hurried over to me, still breathless and laughing about our prank. Short, with round red cheeks, big blue eyes, and curly black hair, she had the look of an adorable doll. She always seemed in a good humor, and as long as I'd known her—from the moment we first arrived at Mrs. Ardel's building—she'd never said a mean word.

Maria was the only one who was kind to me my first day of school, when I was five years old and had just arrived from Odessa, in the Ukraine. The teacher held up a knife and asked us what the word for it was. I called out *"messer,"* Yiddish for "knife." The entire class, including the teacher, burst out laughing. From that moment on, I refused to speak anything but English, even at home. In fact, I still speak English at home while Papa and Mama speak Yiddish back to me.

Maria had been born in New York, so she knew English very well. She helped me a lot that first year. *Perhaps I should choose her first, after all*, I thought, remembering how good she'd been to me.

"Rosie!"

"Yes?"

It was Abe. "You see, you've wandered off again in your mind, and really you mustn't. It's time for the coin toss."

"Who has a coin?" Morris called.

Benjamin raised his hand and showed us a penny.

"Heads," I called.

"Tails," Morris declared.

The coin spun up in the air, then fell at my feet. I bent down. Heads! And before I had even straightened up, I called out, "Isaac!" I didn't look at Maria.

Morris picked next. "Abe!"

So Abe would not be on my team. Fine.

"Peter," I called.

"Stephen," said Morris.

"Max," I announced.

And so it went. I chose Maria as my fifth pick. Finally we were done and ready to start our game. The wind was biting through my sweater and I was anxious to be moving. We tossed the coin once more. I called heads again, but bad luck; it landed tails and we lost the toss. So we were to be the pursuers. We all crowded into the square that Peter had drawn earlier with chalk.

"Maria, you'll be the guard," I stated. She couldn't move fast, I reasoned, and would be more content than the others to remain in one spot. She nodded and tried to smile. In the meantime the other team members had already scattered and were finding their places to hide. I scanned the street. The houses were off-limits. The rule was that you had to hide on the street somewhere. Stoops were allowed too.

I was still standing there, deciding where to run first, when Isaac pulled Hirsch out from behind a shop door. I heard Isaac yell, "Gotcha, gotcha, gotcha!" as he wrapped his arms around Hirsch. Then he began to drag him to our den.

I scampered down the street, pleased that my choice of Isaac had been the correct one. I bent over each pushcart, but since the peddlers stored goods under the carts as well as in them, it was often hard to see anything from there. I heard many of the peddlers complaining. "Hey, you kids, don't you play around here. Bunch of no-goodniks! Outta here!" But we never paid them any mind. The streets were ours just as much as they were theirs, weren't they?

Suddenly I saw a flash of color. Betsy. She was wearing that new scarf, bright pink. I saw it disappear behind a pushcart filled with carrots and onions.

"Cheapest on the street," the old woman was yelling. "The price drops as the sun sets. And good for you too! Hey, lady, come over here," she called to a woman who was looking at vegetables in the next cart over. I tried to ignore the calls and concentrate on finding Betsy when a piercing shriek caught my attention.

"Thief! Thief!"

For a split second everyone stopped and looked. Who had been robbed? Then Mrs. Fishbine came out of her shop like an evil monster, arms waving, face purple, screaming, "Thief! Thief!"

I saw him right away. He was coming right toward me—a skinny little thing, more dirt than boy, with a cap over his eyes and a loaf of bread under his arm. A policeman ran after the boy, blowing his whistle. Over the whistle, I heard Isaac signal. He had his own distinctive whistle. But even without his signal, I would have known what to do. I make my own decisions about these things. Quick as I could, I motioned to the boy to keep running. I leaped out just as he passed me and found Peter and Joshua doing the same. We started a tussle among the three of us so that as the policeman reached us, we tumbled one over the other. The policeman had to stop to get around us.

"You devils, clear off! Out of my way!"

We did so slowly, first making sure the little boy had enough time to escape.

We hated Mrs. Fishbine. Mrs. Smells Like a Fish, we all called her. She never had a kind word, a treat, or a smile. Mama said she just worked hard and was a good businesswoman. *Why couldn't she give that poor boy a piece of bread?* I thought. I smiled at the policeman as we finally got out of his way. He shook his head. He knew quite well what we had done.

And then I saw Betsy! Still hiding where I'd spotted her before. Slowly I knelt down and then crept behind her. She was staring out to the street instead of behind her. It was going to be an easy grab. "Gotcha, gotcha, gotcha!" I screamed as I threw my arms around her. Unfortunately, I scared her so much, she shot straight up and shook the entire cart. Onions and carrots spilled all over the street.

"Oy vay!" the pushcart owner, whom I didn't know, started to scream. *"Szhlok! Szhloken!"*

I knew very well that the peddler was calling us "nincompoops." But what to do? Help her with the vegetables, or keep hold of Betsy? I needed to think fast.

"Betsy," I said, "I'll make you a deal. I'll let go of

you long enough for us to help this old lady, but you have to let me catch you again."

Betsy would have none of it. "Let go of me and it's for good," she declared.

Well, I didn't have a choice, did I? I'd vowed to win. So I dragged her off to the den, the woman screaming after us, *"Szhloken! Oy!"*

I finally got Betsy into the den, but just as I did, Abe—of all people!—popped up from nowhere, jumped with both feet into the den, tagged Betsy, yelled, "Ring-a-levio!" and sprinted off, Betsy right behind him!

If I hadn't been brought up properly, I'm sure I would have cursed. Instead, I spun around and ran after them.

Chapter 2

I HAD ALMOST CAUGHT UP WITH BETSY WHEN I HEARD PAPA'S voice. It rose above all the other voices on the street. *"Rosie!"*

I froze. What could he want? I was in the middle of a very important game!

"Rosie!"

He was calling me again, so it had to be important. And it was certainly Papa—he had this huge deep voice that was very distinctive.

"Rosie!"

I sighed. I had to answer him. I ran over to Maria, and before I opened my mouth, she said, "We can all hear him, Rosie. You'd best go see what he wants. Don't worry. Isaac can be leader while you're gone."

I grimaced. Of course he could. And do better than me, no doubt. But *I* wanted to be the leader!

I wove my way through the crowds toward

Papa's voice and found him standing in front of our apartment block.

"Rosie," he stated grandly, "we are going to the Royale!"

"Now, Papa?" I asked, my mind still completely in the game.

"'Now, Papa?' What kind of answer is that? You always beg me to take you. Today"—he paused for effect—"is the day!"

I hesitated for a moment and then said, "Papa, could tomorrow be the day? I *do* want to go. Badly. But today I'm captain of our team, and we just began the game. . . ."

"Rosie," Papa said, "you can play any day. Today we go to the Royale!"

It's true I had been begging him for well over a year to take me, just the two of us. I loved the theater, and Café Royale was where all the top actors went for their meals. Papa wanted badly to be as great an actor as Jacob Adler, except he could never get a break. Or that's what he said. He worked as a prompter, at the People's Theatre. His manager told him that he liked his work too much to want to let him go on stage. Really, he was indispensable. He wrote down all the scenes that were improvised, advised the writers, often decided on what plays would be done. He practically ran the theater! But he wanted to be an artist and was always trying.

"Are we eating there?" I asked.

"No, no, of course not. I do have a plan I want to carry out, though. I'm going with or without you. What do you say?" Papa drew himself up and tapped the ground with his black walking stick. He always carried it because he said it made him look more distinguished. I thought he looked distinguished all the time, anyway. He was very tall with thick wavy red hair, a long face, brown eyes with very long lashes, and a smile as wide as his face is long. I always thought he would be striking on the stage.

Suddenly it occurred to me how silly I was being. I had been waiting for this invitation for so long! I was going to drink tea at the Royale and sit next to some of the most famous actors.

"Yes, Papa, of course I'll come," I said, beaming.

"Then run upstairs and wash your face," he commanded. "Can't have you looking like a little ragamuffin."

I barreled into the apartment building and up the stairs. We lived in the rear apartment on the second floor of a five-story building. There were three other apartments on our floor: one next to us in the back, two more in front. We shared a bathroom with Maria's family, who lived next to us. Across the way were Mrs. Yoffeh, the palmist, and Mr. Wolf's family, German Jews. Everyone left their front doors open. As usual, Mrs. Yoffeh was sitting on a straight-backed chair, her Ouija board laid out on a small round table that was covered in a lace cloth.

"Surprises in store," she called to me.

"When aren't there, Mrs. Yoffeh?" I called back.

She was always saying strange things to me, but I never paid her any mind. Mama, being a socialist and not believing in religion at all, always told me to ignore her, because fortune-telling was nothing but a way to make money. "You have to admire her enterprising spirit, though," Mama said. When I asked Mama what telling the future had to do with religion, she said, "Think, Rosie dearest. If our future is preordained, there must be someone who is directing it."

I had to admit that made sense.

I hurried into our apartment, where Mama was waiting for me.

"I hear you are going for a treat. The Royale, no less! Here, you may wear this." Mama held out her good black sweater.

"Mama, really?"

"No, I'm teasing. Of course really! Speaking of restaurants, did you hear the one about the deli on Broadway?"

"No, what?" I didn't even roll my eyes. Mama always had a joke.

"When it burned down, the patrons said that was the first time they were ever served hot food!"

As Mama laughed at her own joke I went into the kitchen and scrubbed my face and my hands. Mama followed and helped me off with my sweater. I then pulled her beautiful black one on.

"*Oy*, your boots," she exclaimed. "Look at the state they're in!" She grabbed a *shmata* and rubbed them as well as she could. I straightened my belt, smoothed my skirt, and then felt my hair. Of course it had fallen out of its braids and was sticking out every which way. But Mama already had her brush out. She could braid faster than anyone. In no time, she had pulled the knotted curls as straight as she could and had given me one braid, which hung almost to my waist.

"Hurry now," she said. "Your papa is intent on carrying out his plan today. I have a meeting to go to, so it'll be up to you to feed the children when you get home. Joe is next door. I've bought chicken and potatoes, a loaf of bread, and a piece of butter.

Put the chicken and potatoes on as soon as you and Papa get back."

"Yes, Mama."

"You look lovely."

"Thank you, Mama." Mama always told me in one breath that looks were unimportant and that women had to be fighters for their rights and shouldn't be concerned about such things as appearance. But in another breath she'd tell me what beautiful big brown eyes I had, how my face was so well proportioned, how straight my teeth were, how perfect my little nose was, and what a beautiful red my hair was; and then she'd add, "Not that any of that matters, of course!" Well, I suppose she was right—that looks really don't matter—but compliments are always nice, aren't they? So I never pointed out to her that she was saying two different things at once, in case it made her stop.

I rushed down the steps, two at a time. As soon as I was back on the street, Papa took my hand and we proceeded to the café. As we walked Papa explained his plan.

"When we arrive, we must sit on the left side, naturally," he said. "Only famous people may sit on the right. But we will sit as close to the right as possible. Then I will have a little conversation with

Harry, the busboy. I will slip him a nickel. And I will leave."

"Leave, Papa? Will we have had our tea yet? I'm confused."

"No. We'll order our tea, but I'll leave as soon as we've ordered. Then I'll go over to the candy store next door. And I'll telephone the café and ask for myself."

"Why would you do that?"

"Because Harry will walk all around the café calling for me. You will tell him that I've gone on an errand but that I'll be back directly. And when I return, in a very loud voice, Harry will say a theater was calling for me. A Broadway theater manager! Everyone will take notice. You'll see."

It seemed that our little outing was to be a kind of audition for Papa. He never stopped with his plots and schemes. I'd rather stick a needle in my finger than stand on a stage, but as Mama says, "To each his own." I was excited to help him with his plan.

We were passing a small *shul* when Papa was grabbed on the arm by an old man. "Come in, come in," he said. "We need a minyan."

"I'm sorry, I can't be of help today," Papa replied politely, and he gently removed the man's hand from his jacket. As we walked on he said to me, "I'd do nothing but be in *shul* if I said yes to every one of them."

Papa liked to go to synagogue on the High Holidays. He and Mama often quarreled about that. He said it brought back warm memories of the old country and of his parents, still there. But Mama wanted nothing at all to do with religion. Her parents were both dead, and even if they weren't, she thought religion was just another way to keep women from their rights.

"What meeting is Mama going to tonight?" I asked Papa as I thought about this. "A suffragette meeting or a union meeting?" Mama worked for votes for women, as well as for the unions.

"A union meeting," Papa replied. "Now that one factory, the Triangle, has gone on strike, the union is hoping more people will join. They are even talking about a large general strike for the shirtwaist workers. You know Mama—even though there are so few signed up for the union, she never gives up."

"But Maria has just started working at Mama's shop," I said. "She'll be awfully upset if they go out on strike."

"She's left school?" Papa asked, surprised.

I nodded. "She insisted. She's the oldest, Papa, and she wants to help the family."

"Well, don't you get any such ideas," Papa replied.

"No, I won't," I answered, very relieved to hear him say it. The last thing I wanted to do was to leave school.

It took us almost a half hour to get all the way to Twelfth Street and Second Avenue, because the Sunday crowds were so thick everywhere. But finally we arrived. And right away I recognized Jacob Adler and Bertha Kalish sitting with David Kessler, all of them great actors!

Papa walked slowly to a table quite near them. Of course, he stayed to their left.

"You see Mr. Kessler?" he said to me in a low voice as we sat down.

I nodded my head, too awed to speak.

"Well, when he first came to New York, he acted in a play called *The Ironmaster.* He was such an innovator; he wanted acting to become more natural, to do away with the huge gestures and the screaming. He wanted to portray the truth. But when he tried it, the audience laughed at him! So he stopped the show right then and there and challenged the audience to tell him what was wrong. He refused to continue that night!"

I looked at the great actor, even more impressed. To stop the show and force the audience to think

19

about why they insisted on a certain way of acting? He must be very brave.

Papa had no time for more stories. He called over the busboy, Harry, spoke to him in a very quiet voice, then gave him a nickel. Papa winked at me, stood up, and left. I felt quite odd, sitting there all alone. I hoped this wouldn't take too long. Soon the telephone on the wall rang, Harry answered, and then he roamed all over the café calling, "Is a Mr. Lepidus here? Mr. Lepidus! Telephone call for Mr. Lepidus!"

Of course no one answered.

Moments later, much to my relief, Papa returned. As he walked in Harry shouted, "Mr. Lepidus! A producer from Broadway, no less, was calling for you. He has a part for you, Mr. Lepidus." He handed Papa a piece of paper. "Here, I wrote down his name for you!"

Papa bowed graciously as he took the slip of paper. He sat down, smiled, and ordered our tea and apple strudel—my favorite! Just as it arrived Mr. Jacobson from the Talia Theatre walked over to us.

"Mr. Lepidus?"

"Yes, that is I."

"I couldn't help but overhear that you were tele-phoned concerning an acting job. We have never met, but when I heard your name called—well, I had an idea."

He motioned, asking if he could sit.

Papa said, "Please do."

My heart was pounding. Was this Papa's big break? And was I going to have a chance to witness it?

"I know you well from your work at the People's Theatre," Mr. Jacobson began, "and we all admire how smoothly that theater is run. I've also heard about how organized you are and what a good business head you have. You've kept the theater going through difficult times."

Papa smiled.

"I think your talent would be wasted upon the stage, Mr. Lepidus," Mr. Jacobson continued. "I have quite a different proposal for you."

Papa's face fell. But I was curious. Mr. Jacobson had made the effort to come over. Why?

He didn't keep me in suspense for long.

"I have an opportunity to buy two nickelodeons," he said. "I am looking for a partner. I am too busy with my theater to run them. So if you should have the capital to invest, I propose for us to go in as equal partners, with you running the operations."

Papa was so stunned he didn't answer.

"I know this is like a thunderbolt from above." Mr. Jacobson smiled. "But I have been trying to think of whom to approach to go into this business venture with me, and when I heard your name, it seemed a sign from heaven."

"But," Papa protested, "you don't really know me. Nor I, you. And to go into business together . . . No offense, but there must be trust."

"You are right," Mr. Jacobson agreed. "So let us waste no time. Will you join me for dinner here, now? As my guest, of course. We will spend all evening discussing; we will get to know each other. And then we will see. . . ."

Dinner! Was I to be included?

"Please, if your daughter would like to enjoy a meal with us, she must stay too," he offered.

My heart leaped.

"No, no," Papa said. "It's best if we talk frankly, man to man. Rosie, you eat your strudel and then go home. Mama is expecting you."

I sighed. Too good to be true. Ah, well. I was sitting with a famous producer and I was about to bite into an apple strudel. I was happy for that much.

Little did I know at that moment how much my life was about to change. "It's true what Mama says: No one knows what tomorrow will bring."

Chapter 3

By the time I got home, Mama had already left. Abe wandered in.

"*Nu?*" I asked. "What happened?"

"Your team has six prisoners, including me." Abe sighed. "But our team still has four free," he added, brightening. "We're to play tomorrow after school."

I hurried next door to Maria's to collect Joe. Joe, who was seven, was playing with his friend Matteo and Matteo's older brother, also named Joe.

As I walked onto the landing, Mrs. Yoffeh called to me. "Rosie, Rosie, I see something hovering around your house like a dark cloud."

"Don't say that, Mrs. Yoffeh. You'll bring the evil eye on us," I joked. Of course, I didn't believe in the evil eye, but Mrs. Yoffeh did.

"Never mind, Rosie, you aren't to worry. The angel of death isn't here. Not yet. Not yet."

"Well, that's a relief," I replied. And although I didn't believe her at all, I didn't like the sound of what she was saying.

I didn't have to go to any trouble over Joe. Once back in our apartment, he settled himself in the kitchen on a small comfy chair Mama had found for him. Joe was so different from me and Abe. Only seven, but his nose was always in a book! I mean, I liked my books too, but I'd rather run around outside if given a choice. Not Joe. He'd curl up in a corner and read and read. And when he talked, it was like talking to a grown-up—big words and long sentences!

As I peeled the potatoes I remembered how Mama had introduced Joe to reading, the same way she did it with me and Abe. She sat him down with his first book—his very own, not from the library— and dripped honey on it. When he licked the honey off, she said, "Now you'll remember how sweet learning is."

When Joe was little, he was quiet, too. Mama used to say to me, "Not like you, Rosie." And then Papa would add, "Or like me, when I was a baby."

Papa's name was really Samuel, but he'd screamed so much as a baby that his parents called him Royter—"red" in Yiddish—and eventually that became Roy. "You were just like I was as a baby," he'd say to me. "Red hair, red face. What a temper!"

I did have a temper. I tried to control it, but it got me in trouble. But tonight I had far too much to do to get into trouble. While waiting for the dinner to cook, I ironed the clothes for the next day. Shirt-waists for me and Mama, shirts for Papa and the boys. Luckily, Mama had already boiled the shirts in starch earlier, so I only had to iron them.

After that I fed the children and then washed up the dishes. When all this was finally done, my eyes wanted to close. But I still had my schoolwork: reading poetry for the next day. I loved poems because they were short and expressive *and* I could read them quickly!

I put the boys to bed on their mattresses in the front room. I slept on a mattress in the kitchen. This was the best spot to sleep, really, because it was the warmest. Papa and Mama slept in their own room, but usually Joe would creep into bed with them.

When we first arrived here, we always had boarders. They would put chairs together in the kitchen and sleep on them. The little they paid for rent bought us food until Mama was able to get a full-time job in the factory, sewing, and Papa found work in the theater.

Just as I finished reading my poetry Papa rushed

in, rummaged in the very back of the kitchen cabinet, and drew out a pouch. He gave me a kiss on the cheek and said, "It's a sure thing, Rosie! Even better than me going on the stage!"

And he was gone.

Was that pouch filled with our savings? Had he agreed to Mr. Jacobson's proposal in such a short time? Shouldn't he ask Mama? Just as I was thinking this Mama came in. I knew right away something was wrong.

"Mama!" I exclaimed.

She staggered a little. Her complexion, normally pale against her black hair, was so pale that she almost looked like a ghost—except for two red spots on her cheeks.

"I just need to sit down, Rosie," she assured me.

I put the kettle on for tea.

"What a meeting we had." She smiled as she sank down onto a chair. "We're organizing a big rally at Cooper Union. Big. A general strike, that's what we're working for, Rosie." Her eyes glittered. "Imagine all the workers walking out together. Let those exploiters laugh at us then!"

Just then she began to cough and cough, unable to catch her breath. I ran to get her a glass of water.

"Mama," I said, "you're ill!"

"Nonsense."

"You haven't been well since . . . you know," I said. "You promised Papa you would not work so hard for the union. It's enough that you're at the shop all day, with all of us to look after!"

"Rosie, there are only one hundred of us in Local Twenty-five. I can't stop now. I'm doing this so I won't have to work so hard later. And so you won't either."

I'd heard this often enough.

"I know, Mama, but ever since . . ."

"Rosie, you can say it. Ever since I was beaten. Beaten by the gorillas sent by those owners. Beaten for doing nothing but standing with my sisters on the picket line, standing beside them, supporting them. You don't know what it's like there, Rosie."

She began to cough again.

"I know, Mama. Come. Lie down. Please." I touched her hand. It was dreadfully hot.

"Mama, you're burning!"

"Am I?"

Where was Papa? As I remembered I almost stopped breathing. Papa was off doing something dangerous, and Mama was sick. This couldn't be good.

Hadn't Mrs. Yoffeh warned me about something bad happening?

Mama kept coughing. I took her to her room, helped her undress, and put her nightdress on her. I tucked her in, then hurried next door to fetch Maria's mother.

Mrs. Vaccaro came as soon as I asked her. She leaned over Mama, felt her forehead, listened to her cough, then shook her head.

"She sick," she said to me in English. "Doctor. She weak," she added.

It was true. Since that beating, when she'd broken a rib and had to go to the hospital, she had lost weight and been weak. I bit my cheek. What to do?

"Papa will be home soon," I said.

She nodded, then went to the kitchen. She quickly came back with a cool, wet cloth. "You put on here." She motioned to Mama's forehead. "Every few minutes. And she needs drink."

She had to go back to her children.

I found a lemon and squeezed a bit into a glass of water. I made some tea, too. And I kept putting a cold cloth on Mama's forehead. She tossed around and kept talking to me about the union, and I kept trying to shush her.

Finally Papa came home. "Celia," he called. "Do I have news!"

"Papa!" I ran out to him. "Mama, she's sick."

"Sick?" He hurried into their bedroom. Abe was up by then, and so was Joe. Mama's coughing had woken them. The boys sat quietly, anxious, not saying anything.

"I'll fetch Dr. Meltzer," Papa said after one look at Mama. He kissed her on the forehead. "Haven't I told you?" he scolded. "You do too much!"

"No." Mama smiled weakly. "Others do too little."

Papa shook his head. "She's incorrigible," he said to me. And he hurried off.

I sat with her, urging her to sip the tea.

Dr. Meltzer had taken care of Mama when she'd been in the hospital for her beating. Once Papa returned with the doctor behind him, Dr. Meltzer shooed us all from the room, stayed a couple of minutes, then came out shaking his head.

"I'm afraid," he said to Papa, "it's pneumonia."

We were all silent, staring at him, willing him to take his words back. "Give her this tonic," he said, "and try to keep her fever down. She must have fresh air. Leave the window open." He shook his head. "If you believed, I'd tell you to pray."

"I'll pray anyway!" I blurted out.

"So will I," Abe agreed.

Dr. Meltzer patted our heads. "You do that." Then he turned back to Papa. "She can't work," he warned. "She mustn't get out of that bed until I say so. No meetings. No work. Understand?"

Papa nodded. "I understand. But how to make *her* understand?"

"Find a way," Dr. Meltzer ordered. And then he left.

Papa and I took turns sitting with Mama until she fell into a fitful sleep. Papa then looked at me and said, "Rosie, we have a problem."

I knew right away what he meant.

"That was our savings you took before, wasn't it, Papa?"

"Yes. I've invested in those nickelodeons. Starting tomorrow, I run them. In a few weeks, Rosie, I'll start to see profits. But in the meantime, I have to pay the doctor, I have to pay for medicine, I have to find someone to come sit with Mama."

"Abe will have to do that, Papa."

"Rosie . . ."

"I know, Papa. I'll have to work."

"Just for a few weeks, Rosie. Until I get back on my feet."

"I can do anything, Papa, you know that. Don't worry. I'll go to Mama's boss tomorrow."

"Do they work tomorrow? Saturday?"

I nodded. "Maria was complaining that she had to work all weekend. Something about a big order coming in. I'll tell him I'm sixteen. I could easily pass for sixteen, you know that. Even at eleven, I'm taller than almost everyone in that factory already. I'll say I can run her machine. And I can."

"All right. Good girl." He paused. "I'm sorry, Rosie. I just don't know what else to do." He paused again. "She'll get better, won't she?"

"Of course she will, Papa," I said fiercely. "We won't let anything happen to her!"

"*We* won't, no." Papa sighed. "But will God?"

"But you don't believe in God, Papa. So you can't blame him for this."

"I blame him for everything," Papa explained. "That's why I don't believe in him!"

I didn't understand that at all, and I was far too tired to try. Papa told me to get some sleep, that he'd sit up with Mama. I went into the kitchen, pulled my mattress out from under the table, and sank into it. Before I knew it, Joe had curled up beside me. "Will she die, like Mrs. Brodsky?" he whispered.

"No!" I answered firmly. "We won't let her."

"Mrs. Brodsky's children didn't want her to die," Joe said. "And she did anyway."

"Well, Mama has too much to do," I argued. "We'll have to remind her of her work. It'll keep her fighting spirit alive."

"Maybe," Joe said doubtfully. "But Papa says that's what made her ill."

"Joe, you go to sleep," I said sternly. "Or we'll get sick too."

"Can I stay here with you?" he asked.

"Of course," I said, happy for the company. And although I was so worried, I fell asleep in no time.

Chapter 4

THE NEXT MORNING I WENT TO THE FACTORY WITH MARIA. It was only a short walk, a few blocks down on Orchard Street. The small shop was owned by Mr. Berger, a Jew who'd come here from Germany many years ago. The boss of the factory was named Gold, which I thought was kind of funny.

As we walked up the stairs to the third floor of the factory, Maria warned me, "He is not funny, Rosie. You must be very polite, obey the rules, and *never* make trouble."

Maria was working illegally as a trimmer. All day she would cut the loose threads off the shirts.

"I won't make trouble," I said.

"No outbursts," Maria warned me.

"I know!" I snapped at her.

She gave me a "you'll see" look.

"All right already," I sighed. "I'll be good. I just hope I can keep up with the work."

Maria patted my arm. "You're almost as good on the machine as your mama," she assured me. We walked through the open door, and before she punched her time card, she pointed out Mr. Gold to me. He stood, arms folded, watching the girls as they punched in. He was a small old man with a bald head.

"And who is this?" he asked as I walked up to him.

"Please, Mr. Gold," I said, "my name is Rosie Lepidus. My mother is Celia." I smoothed down the long skirt I had "borrowed" from Mama—without telling her—and tried to appear calm.

"Oh, yes? And? Is there a point to this?"

"Mama is very ill. I'd like to take her spot while she is away."

He opened his mouth in what I presumed was a smile, although he looked more like he was baring his teeth at me.

"And why on earth would I do that? Your mother is nothing but trouble. Good riddance is what I say."

"Because," I said quickly, staring down at him, "because she *is* a troublemaker. And if I were you I wouldn't want to get her mad. Just let me work in her place. It'll be easier for all of us."

The smile dropped off his face. "Well, well, the apple doesn't fall far from the tree, does it?"

I decided it was time to be nice. "I'll work hard, Mr. Gold, I promise. What do you have to lose? You won't miss a day looking for a replacement. And I'm almost as good as Mama. Not as fast, but I'm accurate and neat."

"How old are you?"

"Sixteen."

"All right, then," he said with a grimace. "We'll try it out."

What a relief. "Thank you, Mr. Gold," I said. "Where shall I go?"

He found Mama's card for me, showed me how to punch it in, and pointed out her machine. There were six rows of tables as close together as they could be. There were five tables to each row, and Mama's machine sat in the middle of the third row. The other women were already bent over their machines.

It was a shirtwaist factory, making the kind of ladies' blouses we were all wearing. I tentatively sat in front of Mama's machine and wondered what to do. I looked over to my right and saw an older woman of about thirty bending over her machine, working quickly.

"Hello," I said.

She didn't reply.

I turned to my other side. A younger woman, perhaps seventeen or eighteen, was also bent over her machine. Her brown hair was pulled into a neat bun, and she was dressed in a simple white blouse and a brown skirt. She was bent over her machine, working at an amazing rate.

"Hello," I tried again.

"Shh," she whispered.

"I'm just wondering if you could help me get started. . . . I'm Celia's daughter."

She looked up sharply, then looked toward the boss, who was staring at us both. He was holding a book in his hands, pen over it, ready to write.

She pressed her lips together and bent back over her machine.

I was about to say something nasty when I suddenly remembered something Mama had once told me. She was always ranting and raving about bad working conditions, and I barely listened. But I was sure she'd said something once or twice about the bosses fining the workers for every little thing, even talking. And then I remembered she'd also said they charged workers for the machines they used if they didn't have their own, the needles, the thread—even the chairs they sat in!

What had I gotten myself into? How was I going to do this without help?

"Listen quickly." It was the young woman next to me. The boss, I noticed, had walked over to another table and taken his eyes off us.

"You do the sleeves. When you've finished one, you pass it over to Lottie. She does the collars. Can you do sleeves?"

"Yes," I answered. I looked at the pile already on my table, my heart sinking. "How many do I need to finish?" I asked.

"All of them by lunchtime," she replied.

I felt like giving up right then and there. But we needed the money and I at least had to try. I glanced back at Maria. She sat on the floor at the back of the shop snipping with her scissors.

I took the material, bent over my machine, and began to work. I didn't like it when I saw the boss lock the door to the hallway.

"Why is he doing that?" I whispered under my breath to the young woman next to me.

"So no one can leave without him knowing," she whispered back. "They think if we can leave on our own, we'll steal something."

I hated being closed in. Hated it. I thought about running free in the streets yesterday and longed for that again. Even school seemed more free than this, and I'd always thought being trapped in a classroom felt a bit like being in prison. But this was *truly* like being in prison.

The boss walked over to me.

"If you don't hurry up," he threatened, "all the girls waiting for those sleeves will have no work. And it'll be your fault if they don't earn today. They'll agree with me when I fire you *and* your mother."

I wanted badly to answer him back. In fact, rather than answer him I wanted to hit him on the head with my chair. But I didn't. I bent over the machine and thought, *I'll show him!* And show him I did. Once I put my mind to it, I flew through the sleeves.

After a couple of hours I had to use the bathroom. I asked both my neighbors where it was, but they wouldn't answer me because Mr. Gold was looking at us. So I called him over, the heat rising to my face, and told him I had to go to the bathroom.

"Get up, then," he said.

What was he doing?

"Come with me."

I didn't want him to go with me. How embarrassing!

But he did! He took me to the back of the room. There was a small cloakroom with lockers and, off of that, a door. The minute I opened it, I shrank back from the stench, but I didn't want to let Mr. Gold see me flinch. I hurried in and shut the door. As I was just about to begin I heard a rap on the door.

"Yes?" I said tentatively.

"Hurry up!" Mr. Gold yelled.

As soon as he yelled at me, I found myself unable to do anything, even though I desperately had to.

"Hurry up!"

Finally I gave up. I opened the door to see him standing there, hands on hips, glaring at me. "You'll get us all behind," he chided me.

I had to bite my lip to stop myself from saying anything. I followed him back to my machine, sat down, and spent a miserable couple of hours working, trying not to think about my discomfort.

Finally a bell rang and the girls began to get up. I bolted from my chair toward the bathroom, only to find, once there, that I was fifth in line. When I came out, I looked at the clock to see how much time I had left to eat my lunch. It had been exactly noon when the bell rang. The clock now read 12:20.

But I could not have been in line more than ten minutes.

Maria hurried over to me. She saw me staring at the clock. "Mr. Gold speeds the clock up over the lunch hour, then slows it down once we're back at work," she said.

"He can't do that!" I exclaimed.

"He can do what he likes," she corrected me. "Come. Let's eat."

I sat down with her in a corner, and we quickly devoured the rolls we had brought with us. Also, we each had an orange.

"How are you managing?" Maria asked.

"I can do the work, I think," I replied. "But it seems as if it's a dreadful place." Juice from my orange trickled down my wrist. I licked my fingers. Just then the bell rang, and I heard Mr. Gold shout, "Inspector!"

"Oh no!" Maria said.

Mr. Gold was by her side. "Hide in there," he instructed her, pointing to a large box lying on its side. "As for you," he said to me, "get in the bathroom and stay there."

I didn't hesitate but did as I was told. So he knew I wasn't sixteen and that, like Maria, I shouldn't be working there.

The odor of the bathroom was unbearable. As the minutes passed I was sure I was going to be sick. At least, I supposed, I was in the right place should that happen! Finally Mr. Gold rapped on the door—and this time it was a welcome relief. I entered the workroom to see the women at the machines and Maria on the floor, out of her box. The inspector had left.

I sat down and got back to work. I was concentrating so hard that I jumped when Mr. Gold, from behind my table, yelled, "Stop that!"

"What?" I said, the needle narrowly missing my finger.

"You're singing."

"So?"

"So, it's not allowed. Unless you want to be fined for a half day's work."

I turned back to my machine. No talking, no singing? This was torture!

By the end of the day I had managed to do about three quarters of the sleeves Mama normally did.

"If you don't improve," Mr. Gold stated, "you'll be replaced."

"I'll improve," I assured him.

Maria helped me punch out, then took my hand and led me outside. My back ached, my hands were cramped, my shoulders were sore, and I had a dreadful headache. The workroom had gotten more and more stuffy as the day had gone on, and yet it managed to be cold at the same time. There had, in fact, been nothing good about the entire day.

Maria and I hurried home, worry about Mama at the forefront of my mind. But when we got close to our apartment, Isaac caught sight of me and Maria and called, "Come on! Just two more to catch." Our game of ring-a-levio was still in progress.

"I have to go home," I called back.

"Go in a few minutes," he yelled. "We need you!"

That was all the encouragement necessary, for the truth was, I really didn't want to face the worries of home. I raced down the street looking for someone to capture. I saw Martha right away. She was one of the best at hiding because she was so small. I caught a glimpse of her slipping in between two pushcarts. She wouldn't escape me!

I slowed down, pretended I didn't see her, and sauntered slowly toward the pushcarts, one full of fish, the other, hats. The peddlers were all competing with one another for the very lowest prices since it was so late. A man on horseback was weaving through the crowd, and a horse-drawn buggy was trying to get through as well. I noticed all this as I decided how to best make my catch.

Martha was standing as still as a statue, bent over a hat, as if she were browsing, trying to blend in with the other customers. So that's how she did it! Well, two could play at that. I slowly turned, pretending to look at something on the ground, making sure not to glance her way. In this manner I passed her and then slipped toward the sidewalk on the other side of the fish cart. She was facing toward the street and didn't see me as I crept up behind her. When I was close enough, I threw my arms around Martha and yelled, "Gotcha, gotcha, gotcha!" And then I dragged her triumphantly to the den.

Maria was there waiting for me, a look of disapproval on her face. "Have you forgotten you need to do the shopping for dinner?" she asked, frowning.

"Actually, I had," I said with a groan.

"Come on, I'll come with you," she said.

I looked back at the den with regret. Only one more and our team would win!

"Winning isn't everything," she said.

"Isn't it?" I answered back.

"No, it isn't," she stated firmly.

I loved to compete, and I loved to win even more. In the summer I played stickball with the boys, and I was one of the best players on the team. I could hit and throw farther than any other girl, and most of the boys. Winning was certainly more fun than losing.

Still, Maria was right.

I sighed and put my mind to dinner. I pulled the coins Papa had given me from my skirt pocket. Twenty cents. Well, potatoes, obviously. I could get three pounds for a couple of cents. And if we went to the butcher's, I could get bologna ends and a pumpernickel loaf for a dime. And two herrings for a penny. That would have to do.

By the time we were finished, it was dark. Our feet dragged as we went up the stairs. I got to our apartment in time to see Dr. Meltzer leaving, shaking his head.

My throat closed; I felt a chill run over me.

"She's not dead! She's not dead!" I screamed.

"Rosie. *Shah*!" he said. "No, she's not dead. But her fever is high. If she can make it through the next few days, I'll feel more hopeful."

I rushed into the apartment. Papa was home already, as were the boys. Mama was in her bed with the window open, so the room was terribly cold. She moved restlessly and seemed to be almost gasping for breath.

I turned back to the kitchen, suddenly feeling quite numb. She couldn't die. She couldn't.

Chapter 5

THE NEXT MORNING I COULD HARDLY BEAR TO LEAVE MAMA. At least she was no worse, although that was saying little. At times she breathed in this shallow way, almost as if she'd been running. The coughing fits she had were pitiable. We couldn't get her to eat, but we all took turns making sure she was drinking.

Maria had to pull me away from Mama's bed. She waited for me to change into the long skirt, and then hurried me out of the apartment. When we arrived at work, we punched in. I found the work easier that day, but felt like I might die from boredom. Forbidden to sing or even hum, not being allowed to talk with my neighbors while I worked—it was almost impossible! Mama had taught me to be such a good machinist by making sure I was never bored. We would sing songs as I practiced, make up little plays, chatter, do riddles.

That way, I didn't mind the endless hours at the machine.

It had been a huge expense to own a machine. Papa arranged to pay twenty-five cents a week and it would take eighteen years to pay it off, but it was worth it when Mama could get piecework to do at home. When she finally got the job at the factory, she took in her own machine, so she didn't need to rent one from the owner.

By the time our lunch break arrived, I honestly thought I might cry from relief. All the girls—I'd say at least three quarters of those working there were between sixteen and twenty—gathered around the young woman who worked next to me, Jenny. She had a newspaper, the *New York Times*, and was showing it to everyone. The front-page story was about the shirtwaist workers!

"It tells of our terrible working conditions," she whispered. "It tells of everything."

"And the strike?" a girl asked.

"Yes, it tells of the Triangle strike. This paper ignored the strike until a lady, a Miss Mary Dreier, became involved. She was arrested when she was standing on the Triangle factory picket line. It says here the police have apologized for arresting her."

"They never apologized to my mama," I exclaimed, "for not protecting her. They stood by and watched as she was beaten."

The girls all remembered, of course, because Mama had told them about it when she returned to work after being in the hospital.

"Well, your mama isn't a lady from the Upper East Side," Jenny said.

"To think," another girl said, "that all of New York is reading about us."

"So this is the time for a general strike," Jenny said. And from the way she said it, I thought it probably wasn't the first time they'd had this conversation. She spoke with a serious demeanor, which seemed natural to her, intensely focused on getting her point across.

"If one of us asks for better working conditions, we know nothing will happen," she continued, "because so many of us have tried that. But if we all do . . ."

"Shah," said another girl. She put her hand on Jenny's arm as a warning, because Mr. Gold was walking toward us. Jenny folded the paper and tucked it into the back of her skirt. We all moved away and went to eat.

The afternoon passed even more slowly than the

morning. There was one break in the monotony when a girl stuck her finger with a needle. We all jumped as her scream shattered the deathly silence, but she wound a cloth around her finger and continued. She would receive no time off for her injury and no help from the boss, so she had to pretend it wasn't serious.

Just as I was counting the seconds to closing time, Mr. Gold announced that we would have to put in three more hours to meet the quota. I looked around, waiting for someone to object. No one said a word! And then I thought of all the times Mama had been home late from work and I'd had to fix dinner. This probably happened often. Just thinking about having to sit for three more hours made my legs itch to move. Suddenly I had to stretch. I just *had* to. I got up from my machine, stretched my arms and my legs, and bent over. When I straightened up, Mr. Gold was standing over me.

"That'll cost you the last three hours of your work."

"Why?"

"Because just as singing and talking are punishable by fines, so is stretching."

"But that isn't fair!"

"Are you going to talk back to me?"

"Why the last three hours? Why not the next few hours?"

He did that thing that was supposed to be a smile. "You aren't paid extra," he said, then turned his back on me.

So we were to work the next few hours for free? And I was to be fined for standing up? But people must have to stand all the time. Or talk. And then I suddenly understood. These were just more rules he had made up so he could pay us less. And any excuse to pay us less would do. I was so angry, I must have turned bright red, because Jenny leaned over, pulled on my skirt, and plunked me back on my chair.

"Why doesn't everyone quit?" I muttered. "Why stand for this?"

She raised her eyebrows and patted the back of her waist, where she'd tucked away the newspaper. Recalling what the article said, it became clear to me why Mama was always so upset. It just wasn't fair! And it wasn't as though all these women could quit, because nowhere else was any better. That's why all the factory workers had to stick together. If everyone went on strike, the owners would have to agree to the workers' demands, wouldn't they? All of Mama's ranting now made sense.

I was really angry. I vowed, right then and there, right at that moment, that I would do whatever I could to help the union and the strikers.

It wasn't until seven thirty that evening that we were finally allowed to go home. Maria and I walked down the stairs together. As we did we passed an open door. Through it, I saw rows and rows of tables packed with men who were cutting out patterns. It was even more crowded than our floor. Perhaps we were lucky: A sewing machine station took up a certain amount of room, and space had to be allowed for that.

Hand in hand, Maria and I hurried home in the dark. As we raced up the stairs Mrs. Yoffeh called to me. "Didn't you promise to pray?"

I stopped dead on the landing. "How did you know that?" Goose bumps crawled over my skin.

"It's time to keep your promise, little Rosie," she said.

I backed away from her door, now truly afraid. Was it possible that Mama had been wrong all along about religion?

Maria whispered to me. "Is it true?"

I nodded.

"Then you better pray."

"I don't know how."

"Come over after you've eaten. I'll help you." Maria and her family were Catholic, and they went to church regularly and lit candles at home.

"I will," I agreed.

Still shaken, I hurried into our apartment, dreading to find Mama worse—and, in fact, she was. I knew it as soon as I entered the apartment. There were no children playing. I could see that my brothers weren't there at all. Papa must have sent them over to Mrs. Vaccaro's for dinner. I crept into the back room. Mama was tossing and turning, and Papa was sitting beside her with a look of such helplessness on his face, it took my breath away. I'd never seen Papa look like that. He was always so busy, running around, "bringing culture to the world," as he would say, that I never thought anything could stop him. When he saw me, he seemed to put on a mask, like those that were sometimes used at his theater. He smiled at me, as if to say, *Don't worry,* but that made me worry even more.

"You'd best go stay at Maria's tonight," he said.

"But Papa, I want to be here with you. I can

make you and Mama tea. Have you eaten?"

He looked like he was forcing himself to stay calm, to not get angry with me. "Rosie," he said slowly, "go to Maria's."

I backed out of the room and ran over to Maria's. When she greeted me at the door I was so upset that I wanted to scream or hit something or . . . or . . . I don't know. I just didn't want Mama to die!

Maria took my hand. "Come."

The boys were playing a game of marbles together in the kitchen. The men were at the kitchen table playing cards. Mrs. Vaccaro, as usual, was cleaning. Her apartment was spotless at all times. Naturally, Mama kept our home clean too, but she was so busy with work and meetings that, well, it was never quite as clean as Maria's.

We went into the front room and Maria kneeled in front of the picture of the Virgin Mary. I knew she often prayed to the picture. She motioned me to kneel beside her.

"Is it all right for a Jew to pray to the Virgin Mary?" I asked.

"Of course," she said. "She'll help anyone!"

"I don't know who to pray to otherwise. I mean, Jewish-wise," I admitted. "Maybe God?"

"Let's pray to her first. Then to God."

That made sense to me. Maria started to recite a prayer. She said it very fast and under her breath, and she seemed to know exactly what she was doing. I felt envious. I wished I could simply talk to someone in heaven like that. I wished I could believe in something like that. On the other hand, it wasn't so much that I didn't believe, I just had never been encouraged to think about it at all. But sometimes I found myself doing just that, because the more Mama would say religion was silly, the more I would wonder. For instance, I would ask, "Well, if there is no God, how did we get here?" And Mama would say, "Evolution. We evolved from the lower species. It's all accidental." But then I would sit on the fire escape, and I would marvel at the leaves on the trees, if it was summer, or at the snowflakes drifting past my nose, if it was winter, and I would think, *But these are all miracles. Could they happen by accident?*

Maria turned to me and took my hand. She seemed to be finished with her prayer. "Think what you'd like to say to God," she said.

I thought for a moment. "All right. I've thought."

"Good. Now bow your head and start with 'Dear God,' and then say what you want to say."

"Dear God," I said, "please don't let Mama die. I

don't know whether or not you can hear me, but if you can, and if there is a heaven, please don't take Mama there. We need her here. And not just me and Papa and the boys. She has lots of work to do for other girls who are working very hard and are very miserable. So, all in all, there's no good reason to take her and many good reasons to leave her."

I stopped.

"Now say, 'Amen,' " instructed Maria.

"Amen," I said. And then I begged, fervently, "Please. Please. God, Please."

I looked at Maria. She nodded and kissed my cheek. "We can pray again later tonight," she promised, "before we sleep. Now let's get some food."

We went into the kitchen, where Mrs. Vaccaro gave us some noodles with tomatoes that she had cooked earlier. I loved eating at Maria's house. The food was always delicious. Mama cooked to feed us, but Mrs. Vaccaro cooked to make people happy. And the food did make me feel better.

After we'd eaten I crept back to our apartment and to Papa. He was asleep in the chair by Mama's bed, but she was awake. I hurried to the kitchen, made Mama some tea, stirred honey into it, then took it to her. She didn't seem to recognize me as she tossed and turned. I sat her up, and she allowed me to spoon-feed her the tea. Then suddenly she grabbed my wrist. "Rosie. Rosie."

"Yes, Mama?"

"You'll look after Papa, won't you?"

"Mama, I always do."

"No. No. If I die."

I looked in her eyes then and tried to hold on to my anger. "Mama," I said firmly, "you are not going to die. Do you hear me? I won't allow it. We need you, and . . . and, well, it looks like there is going to be a general strike. Do you want to miss out on that?"

She looked at me, surprised. "No," she said uncertainly.

"Well, then, you'd best hurry up and get better. And besides that," I said, thinking this could shock her into getting better, "I prayed tonight. To God."

"Rosie!" Papa said, waking. "Are you trying to upset her?"

"No, Papa," I said. "I'm trying to force her to get better."

"All right, Rosie, that's enough. You've tired her out. Look, she's . . ." He looked at her. "She's sleeping."

She did seem to be sleeping. Not tossing and turning, but in a deep sleep.

"Is that good, Papa? Or bad?"

"I don't know. I'm going to get Dr. Meltzer."

He ran out and left me with Mama. After a few minutes Abe crept in and sat on the floor. Joe did the same. When Papa came home with Dr. Meltzer, we were all there, sitting, not saying a word.

Dr. Meltzer signaled us to leave the room. We waited in the kitchen. Papa paced up and down the tiny space. Abe and Joe silently pushed a marble back and forth across the table. I stood there motionless, every minute feeling like forever. At last Dr. Meltzer came out, a smile on his face.

"She's sleeping peacefully. I believe the worst is over. Now, do not let her do *anything*. For at least two more weeks."

Tears streamed down my face. Abe and Joe threw themselves into my arms, and then Papa hugged us all.

"Thank you, God," I whispered.

Chapter 6

I WOKE UP THE NEXT MORNING EXHAUSTED AND NOT QUITE believing that Mama was truly going to get better. She was still coughing terribly in the back room. When I hurried in to see her, though, she was sitting up in bed and actually eating a little mashed banana Papa had made for her.

She smiled when she saw me and patted the bed. I sat down.

"You have a very interesting bedside manner," Mama commented. "I think you scolded me into getting better."

"Truly?" I asked, feeling quite pleased.

"Truly. I was *afraid* to die after you'd finished your little lecture!"

I kissed her forehead. "Mama, I have so much to tell you!"

"Not now," Papa ordered as he came back into the room. "Mama needs to sleep. You go." He gave me a look as if to say, *And don't mention where you are going.* "You can tell your mama all your news later. Perhaps tomorrow. . . . We'll see."

Oh, I realized, *Mama still knows nothing of what's happened. The nickelodeons, my working, nothing.*

"Abe will stay home with you again today," Papa said to Mama. "You just try to sleep."

"No, let him go to school," Mama objected. "I'll be fine."

"Tomorrow," Papa said firmly. And when he used that tone, there was no sense in arguing.

I made sure to dress in Mama's long skirt where she couldn't see me. I called good-bye to her when Maria came to fetch me. As soon as we were on the landing, Mrs. Yoffeh called to me. "God heard your prayers."

"Why does he hear some prayers and not others?" I called back, wondering about what Joe had said to me the other night. Lots of children and parents died. Lots. Did God hate some people and love others? That didn't seem to make sense.

She laughed, an odd kind of cackle. "Oh, you're a clever one, you are."

"Well?" I demanded, hands on hips.

"Come closer," she said.

Maria tugged at me. "Do you want to lose a half day's pay? Because that's what'll happen if we're even five minutes late."

I certainly didn't. As I followed Maria down the stairs, I heard Mrs. Yoffeh's voice. "God loves everyone, Rosie."

"Then why do such awful things happen?" I whispered to Maria.

"Because of our sins," Maria answered.

I shook my head. "I respect what you believe, of course," I assured her, "but, really, that makes no sense to me. Mama is not sinful."

"Everyone is," Maria said.

"I need to ask Papa about this," I responded, "because that just doesn't seem right to me."

We were soon at the shop, and all of these thoughts were quickly replaced by the need to concentrate on the work. That morning was as awful as the ones before. Rather than getting used to the silence and the boredom, I was going mad. How on earth did Mama manage, day after day?

Over lunch Jenny again read to us from the *Times,* plus she had big news. "There's to be a meeting," she said, "at Cooper Union tonight. Everyone must come. That's where we'll vote on a general strike."

On the one hand, I felt excited; a general strike was exactly what Mama had been working so hard for. On the other hand, without Mama's wage and Papa's savings how on earth would our family survive?

Just as we returned to our machines there was the most terrible sound, like a thunderclap. Our building shook. My machine rocked and I had to pull my hand out quickly so it wouldn't be caught by the needle. Not all the girls were as lucky. I heard shrieks everywhere, some from fear but most from pain, as needles pierced fingers and thumbs.

Everyone, except those nursing their wounds, leaped up and ran to the door. But it was locked. Mr. Gold was at the back of the room, and he was the only person who could open it. The shaking subsided, but we heard more crashes and screams from outside.

We were trapped!

I was tall enough that I could see Mr. Gold trying to get through the crowd of girls pushed up against the door, but he couldn't do it. I tried to clear the way for him.

"Let him through," I yelled in my loudest Papa-like voice. "Let him through!"

Although panicked, some of the girls from the

back began to help him push his way, echoing my call, "Let him through!" Eventually he made it to the front of the room and was able to unlock the door. Once the door was unlocked, though, he turned to us and yelled, "It's no use. The stairwell is full of people. Stay back! Stay back!" But no one listened. The crush of women at the stairs forced Mr. Gold into the stairwell.

If this is a fire, I thought, *we'll all die here, trapped, burned like animals*. But I didn't smell smoke. A couple of other girls who were too terrified to think straight tried to push their way onto the stairs. Jenny tried to stop them.

"The stairwell will collapse," she warned, "if too many of us get on it. And then we will die for sure. There's no smoke. Let's just wait."

Most were convinced, but a few pushed ahead anyway. The girls from the floor above called to us. "What's happening? What should we do?"

"Wait until it's clear," Jenny called back.

It took at least ten minutes for the stairwell to clear enough for us to try to get down. We spoke to one another in whispers, as if making too much noise might cause another crash. Finally Mr. Gold motioned us to move ahead. I was jostled and pushed as I tried to get down the stairs. A girl ahead of me tripped, and I helped her up. If there had been a fire, we'd certainly all be dead. I shuddered at the thought.

At last we reached the ground floor. As I walked out into the street I moved into a cloud of dust. I waited for Maria at the entrance, then, hand in hand, we tried to discover what had happened. We could hear the police blowing their whistles. But the main sounds we heard were the terrible screams of people in pain. The dust was everywhere, so it was hard to see what had happened. As we pushed our way into the street, though, it became evident: The building next to us had collapsed. That is, part of it had. You could see through the outer wall, which had cracked open, that the second floor had given way and fallen into the first floor. Part of the inner wall had given way too. People were trapped on the stairwell trying to get down. Many people must have been crushed below all the rubble on the first floor.

I heard Jenny's voice behind me, which was calm considering what we were witnessing. "They put so many people to work on each floor. This same thing happened a couple of years ago at the Lipson factory. The same horrors over and over."

"What can we do?" I asked her, turning to see

her standing there, hands on hips, shaking her head. She seemed more angry than upset.

"Maybe we can help the people on the staircase," she replied. She ran over to some of the men from our factory and pointed to where some workers were trapped. It looked like they couldn't get beyond planks that had fallen across a doorway.

In no time, the men started clearing the debris. Others moved into the factory and tried to pull people out. The sound of the fire bells was a welcome noise. More policemen began to arrive too.

I looked at the wreckage.

As if she had read my mind, Maria said, "No, don't. It could fall again."

"I have to." I followed the men into the building. I had to help. I could climb into the room over what was left of the wall through a hole, which was about three feet high and wide enough for a person to squeeze through. I wasn't strong enough to lift planks off people, but there had to be something I could do.

As soon as I got into the room, I noticed some children cowering in a corner. They were no older than me, so they must have been working as snippers. Some had blood on them, but most seemed unhurt—just too stunned and frightened to move. There were six by my count. I helped the smallest up. "Can you walk?"

"I think so."

I took her by the arm and led her through the mass of bodies and machines and wood to the opening in the wall.

"Maria!" I called.

Maria hurried over.

"Get someone to help lift them out."

Maria nodded and turned to find a man who could help.

I went back for another. I tried not to see the wounded, but I couldn't help it. Some bodies were mangled in terrible ways. There was blood everywhere, and pitiable screams of pain were coming from the trapped and injured.

As I was helping the second child a stream of police and firemen rushed in. Thinking I was one of the victims, a fireman pulled me out through the hole and deposited me on the street beside Maria. I have to say that I was relieved. Maria grabbed my hand and pulled me away.

"We're going home," she said firmly.

I didn't argue.

When we were a block away from the horrible

scene, I took a deep breath. "I don't know if I can go back to that job," I said. "Or let Mama go back. Can you imagine what would have happened if that had been a fire?"

"What choice do we have?" she said, not looking at me. "We have to eat, don't we?"

She was right. What choice *did* we have?

But perhaps we did have a choice.

"I'm going to that meeting tonight," I stated. "Want to come?"

Maria shook her head. "Are you serious?"

Her father would never allow it. Although she slipped out to play on the street with us and was allowed to walk to work on her own, even that was far more than her father approved of. She would not be allowed out at night without a male relative. Probably not ever, even when she was married.

"Well," I said, "I'm going to go. When Mama gets better, I can tell her all about it. If there is a strike, maybe the owners won't lock us in anymore. Maybe they'll let us talk when we work. Maybe they won't pack us in so close that entire floors fall in. Maybe we can actually change things."

When we got home, Mrs. Yoffeh was busy with a customer and paid me no mind, something for which I was very thankful. I had done the shopping, so I made dinner for everyone and then made sure Mama was comfortable before I went out. I didn't tell her where I was going; I didn't want her to worry about my being out all alone.

"Did you hear the one about the doctor?" she said to me as I was trying to sneak away. "He took time off work at the hospital to go hunting. When he returned to work, the nurse asked him how he'd done. 'Terrible,' he said. 'I didn't kill a thing.' 'Well then,' said the nurse, 'you would have been better off staying here!'"

I laughed and gave her a kiss. "Now I know you're feeling better," I said.

"Where are you off to in such a rush?" she asked. "Stay here and read to me."

"I can't, Mama," I said. "I promised Molly in the next building over that I'd help her with her reading."

Mama smiled. "Good for you," she said.

I didn't feel happy about lying to her, but I felt that going to this rally was important enough that I had to do it.

I told Papa the same story, and then I hurried away. I made my way as quickly as I could through the busy streets to Cooper Union. It's a huge hall, but it was packed with people. Thousands, I supposed. I squeezed into the back of the crowd.

Men sat on the stage and made speeches in Yiddish. Mostly it seemed like they were saying that the women shouldn't strike. It would be too hard, there would be danger, arrests, even jail. One after another, they got up and repeated their arguments. I felt so disappointed; so there was to be no strike after all? At least we'd have a paycheck, and I did have to be glad about that.

I turned to leave, but just then a thin voice rose above the rest. "I want to say a few words." It was a girl from the crowd. Soon everyone was telling her to get up on the stage. Once she made her way to the front, a number of girls lifted her up onto the stage so she was standing side by side with all the union bigwigs.

The girl was slim, with black hair and a round face. She called out in a loud voice, "I am a working girl, one of those striking against intolerable conditions. I am tired of listening to speakers who generalize. What we are here for is to decide whether or not to strike. I offer a resolution that a general strike be ordered now!"

Everyone around me leaped to their feet. They began to clap and scream, "Yes, yes!" Beside me a woman took off her hat and waved it in the air so she could be seen from the stage. Others were doing the same. Those with no hats waved their handkerchiefs. It was amazing. Everything changed because of the few words this girl spoke.

"Who is that?" I asked the woman beside me.

"That is Clara Lemlich," the woman answered. "A worker, just like us."

Why, she was one of Mama's friends, one of the union workers Mama worked with! I'd heard Mama mention her name many times.

The excitement in the hall seemed to last forever. When it finally quieted down, a man came to the front of the stage. He shouted, "Will someone second the resolution?"

Everyone called, "Yes!" at the same time. The room was electrified. The man took Clara's arm and raised it in the air. "Do you mean it in good faith? Will you take the old Jewish oath?"

Almost all the workers at the factories were Jewish girls. So the entire hall filled with the sound of these girls answering back at the top of their lungs, "Yes! If I turn traitor to the cause I now pledge, may this hand wither from the arm I raise!"

The entire hall then hummed with noise and movement as everyone stopped paying attention to the speakers on the stage and began to talk to one another. Soon people began drifting out of the hall.

I wrapped my sweater around me and hurried outside. It was bitterly cold.

As I walked home I wondered what I should do about the strike.

Papa and Mama would expect me to return to school if I wasn't going to be working. But I didn't want to. Not yet. I wanted to stand on the picket line with the others. I wanted to fight! Fight those horrible bosses and owners so Mama wouldn't have to suffer anymore. If we didn't all fight together, well, it was just a matter of time before Mama would get sick again, wasn't it? Being overworked at the factory and her union work had taken a toll on her. Although we desperately needed Mama's paycheck, how could that be more important than her health?

By the time I was home, I'd made a decision. I wouldn't tell Papa or Mama. Let them think I was going to school.

Mrs. Yoffeh was at her post. "How much courage do you have?" she called to me.

"I don't know," I answered.

"You're about to find out."

Now what? I wondered. But I decided not to stop and ask her. I had quite enough to worry about!

Chapter 7

THE NEXT MORNING I GOT UP AND GOT DRESSED AS USUAL. Papa asked me if I thought the strike would really happen. I said I wasn't sure, but in case it didn't, I would go to work.

Maria called on me as usual, and as we walked I told her everything that had happened at the meeting the night before. I finished my story just as we reached the factory.

"You make it all come alive," she said. "I almost feel as if I were there."

We stood for a moment and stared at the hole in the wall of the building beside us. I could still see blood on the pavement.

"I don't want to go up there," I said to Maria. "What if that happens to us, or what if there's a fire?"

"We have no choice, remember?" Maria reminded me. "No other shop has better conditions, or so Mama tells me. We may as well be here as anywhere."

I took a deep breath and clasped Maria's hand. "Let's go, then," I said. "We can only hope the strike will really happen."

"You can hope," Maria said. "Our family needs the money."

I didn't want to argue with her. My family was even more desperate. Slowly, we climbed the stairs. When we got to the clock to punch in, Mr. Gold was standing there with his notepad speaking to Jenny and the others. "You will be losing a half day's pay, of course, since you didn't work yesterday afternoon," he told us.

"Do you mean," Jenny asked him, "you won't be paying us for yesterday?"

"No," he answered, "I mean I won't be paying you for a half day today as punishment for not working yesterday."

"Mr. Gold," Jenny objected, "that's not at all fair. How could we work after that accident?"

"I'll decide what's fair, Miss Lensky," Mr. Gold said. "Now, do you want to work or not?"

Jenny and the others punched in, and so did I. We started to work. I was in terrible suspense. Would any of them have the courage to stop? To simply stand up and walk out? Or would we continue to work? What was happening in the other shops? Was everyone back to work as usual, or had they walked out as promised last night?

I could barely concentrate on my work, but at least I wasn't bored. And yet the minutes seemed to go by one by one, and I could count each one! And then it happened.

Jenny stood up.

"Miss Lensky, what are you doing?" Mr. Gold called to her from across the room.

"Mr. Gold," she said calmly, "I am on strike."

I admired Jenny so much at that moment. She spoke with that quiet intensity she had, that solemn manner that made everyone want to follow her. One by one, each of the girls stood up and used Jenny's words. "Mr. Gold, I am on strike." "Mr. Gold, I am on strike." Finally I stood up and said, "I'd like to say that, for my mama, I am on strike too!"

At this the other girls broke out in laughter and lifted me on their shoulders! I didn't understand why until Jenny called, "You shall be our good luck charm and come everywhere with us. What do you say, girls?" It was the first time I'd seen Jenny really smile.

"Yes!" they all agreed, clapping and giggling. "As long as young Rosie is with us, we cannot lose!"

I honestly didn't know if they were teasing me because of my age or admiring me for trying to be part of their fight even though I was young. But I supposed that it didn't really matter. I would stand by them because I would never forget Mama's illness and how we almost lost her.

They put me down as we moved toward the stairs. Mr. Gold yelled, "You'll be sorry! You'll regret this, every single one of you! Your jobs will all be gone and . . ."

But the girls ignored his ranting and raving, and we all filed out. Maria slipped her hand into mine, and we hastened down the stairs to the street together. When we got there, we were both astounded by what we saw: The street was crammed with women cheering, singing, and even dancing! Horse-drawn carts and automobiles were stuck, unable to move.

"On to Clinton Hall," the women called to one another. "Join the union so you can picket!" I couldn't join the union at my age, but I knew Mama was already a member. I resolved to go to Clinton Hall in her stead and see what I could do.

Maria stopped and turned toward me. "I must go home, Rosie."

"But come with me first," I asked of her.

"You know I can't," she replied, shaking her head. "Papa would be furious."

"He would," I agreed. "Never mind, I'll tell you everything later," I assured her.

Just then Jenny passed by, caught my arm, and pulled me along with her. It took us over an hour to get to the hall, pushing our way through the crowds, but I didn't care. It was like being at the biggest party in the world. What a feeling there was in the streets! So many girls walking arm in arm, hand in hand, together, beginning on a grand adventure. But soon policemen started to appear and order us to behave.

Behave? What did that mean? Were we not people? Did we not have the right to walk on the street? Were we breaking any laws? I didn't think so, but I saw some of the policemen making threatening motions with their clubs as they tried to clear the way for the buggies, autos, and horses.

Once we finally reached the hall, I squeezed through to the desks and introduced myself to an older woman. "I'm Celia Lepidus's daughter," I screamed over the noise.

"Who?"

"Celia!"

"Her daughter?"

"Yes."

"Where is she?"

"Sick. Can I help?"

"Yes, dear, you certainly can. Can you read and write?"

"Yes."

"Good. Sit here beside me. Union dues are one dollar and fifty cents, but often the women can pay only ten cents a day. You need to help me make the lists of who pays and how much."

I did as she requested. I found a chair, sat down, and began writing names on a long sheet of white paper. The lines of women stretched well outside the door.

I stayed until evening and then had to leave to make dinner for Mama and the boys.

When I reached Orchard Street, I passed Isaac. When he saw me, he grumbled, "We had to stop our game today because there were so many women on the street!"

I grinned. "I know," I said proudly. "I've been with them! We're going to change everything." Then I stuck my nose up in the air. "You can play your childish game anytime." Isaac glared at me as I laughed and hurried away.

I entered our apartment to find Mama sitting in the front room, a blanket round her. She was still coughing, but her eyes were much clearer.

"Mama!" I exclaimed. "You look so much better."

"I am, darling Rosie," she said. "Good tidings can be heard from afar, is that not true?"

"So you know?"

"Of course I know. It's the day I've been working for and waiting for and even, yes, dreaming of! I just *wish* I could have been there."

"It wouldn't have happened if you and the others hadn't worked so hard, Mama," I reminded her. "But I should go out now and buy our supper."

"Abe has done that already," Mama told me, "so you just need to prepare it."

Papa walked in then, bringing with him a can full of beer from the tavern down the street. He told Mama she was to drink a glass before dinner to help get her strength up. Dr. Meltzer's orders.

"I'll try," Mama promised as she took a glass from Papa.

I washed the potatoes and put them on to boil. I put out the bread and the herring. Then I began cleaning the carrots; I'd simmer them with a few raisins and a little honey. Mama loved that dish, and so did the boys.

"Lots of excitement, Rosie," Papa said, speaking low as he stood beside me at the stove. "I've not told Mama about the nickelodeons yet," he added. "I don't want to until she is stronger. She'll worry about the money. And let's not mention your working for those few days yet, either. Still," he added, excitement in his voice, "what with all of the women out of work and the picket lines not yet up, lots of them decided to go see a moving picture. Today we had people lined up for blocks!"

"That's wonderful, Papa!"

"Yes, it is. But even with full houses, we need to invest all the money back into the business, buying new movie reels. I'm not sure when we will see a profit." He paused. "But that's for me to worry about. As for you, tomorrow it's back to school. Correct?"

"Yes, Papa," I agreed. But I had no intention of doing any such thing. I would meet Jenny and the others in front of the shop in the morning.

I remembered, though, that I had something I wanted to ask him. "Papa, I know you and Mama don't believe in God, but can you tell me something? If there *is* a God, why would he let such bad things happen? Maria says it's because we're all sinners. Do Jewish people believe that?"

Papa looked at me thoughtfully for a moment.

"That is a very difficult question, Rosie," Papa said, "because there are so many different beliefs in Judaism. A Reform Jew has very different beliefs from an Orthodox Jew."

"But we're neither, correct?" I asked.

"We're Freethinkers," Papa replied. "We want to break away from all those old religious rules. But we are still Jewish. And I believe that people are basically good, not basically evil. And many Jews believe that. If you follow the central core of Judaism, 'Love thy neighbor as thyself,' well, then, you will be a good person and a good Jew."

"That's what Mama does," I said. "So why did she get sick?"

"Maybe God doesn't decide who gets sick and who doesn't. Maybe it's just accidental."

"Then how can Mrs. Yoffeh predict it?"

"Did she?"

I nodded.

Papa smiled at me. "Rosie, it seems to me that these are things you will have to start to think about and figure out for yourself. Just remember, there is no *one* answer. As you get older, you will have to sort it out."

"But," I replied, "it doesn't sound like you have!"

Papa laughed and mussed my hair. "How right you are."

"What are you two whispering about?" Mama asked.

"Nothing, Mama," I replied, and I turned to concentrate on the dinner.

I dressed the next day in Mama's oldest long skirt, one I didn't think she'd miss, and slipped out without Papa seeing me. The streets were still packed with people as if no one had bothered to go home to sleep. Already there were placards up in English, in Hebrew, and even some in Italian. Pretzel makers hawked their wares, as did women with baskets full of apples. Women were singing and holding up their banners.

I made my way to the shop. The second I spotted Jenny, I hurried over to her.

"Rosie! You haven't deserted us, then?" She used the same serious voice she always did, but I was beginning to realize that there was often a small smile hidden just beneath the surface.

"No!" I declared. "And I won't."

"Well, that's all very well," Jenny said, "but it won't be long before the gorillas arrive—the brutes the bosses hire to beat us and intimidate us. They'll try to scare us off. I don't want you to get hurt. So when that happens, you must promise me to hurry away until it's safe."

I paused for a moment, not wanting to promise any such thing.

"Rosie," she repeated, a stern look on her face.

"All right," I agreed reluctantly.

"Good, then." She turned to the building wall where the placards were stacked and gave me one in English, which read:

STRIKE!

20,000 SHIRTWAIST MAKERS

HIGHER WAGES

SHORTER HOURS

I picked it up and began to pace in front of the building, alongside the other girls. It wasn't long before trouble started. Some of the girls from our shop arrived, but instead of standing outside with us, they went up to work. I couldn't believe it!

"What are they doing?" I asked Jenny.

"They are going to work," she said grimly.

"Scabs!" the women on the picket line began to scream at the other women. I knew from Mama what that word meant. It meant people who would continue to work even when a strike was on or people who were hired to replace the workers out on strike.

And after all, if these women did that, why would the bosses ever recognize the union? Why would they give us *anything*? They could just continue as if nothing had happened!

Huge goons made a path for the scabs, pushing and shoving so they could get through. Suddenly the police were there, and rather than arresting the hired gorillas who were pushing the picketers, they started to grab the women who were picketing! A horse-drawn paddy wagon pulled up, and I could see three of the girls from our shop shoved into the wagon. Then some of the gorillas began to club the girls with their sticks.

"Rosie!" Jenny called.

I shrank back against the wall and tried to get out of the way as I'd promised. But there was nowhere to go. Everyone was screaming and shouting. The policemen were yelling, "Let the workers through! Behave!"

The gorillas were shouting, "Get out of the way. This'll teach you!" and things like that.

The shoving came closer and closer to me until I

saw a huge gorilla, at least six feet tall, with dark eyes and a dark beard raising his club right over my head. Dread shot through me, from the hair on my head to my very toes. And that made me mad, really mad. I raised my banner to the gorilla and threw back my head and looked him in the eyes.

"Hitting girls, that's how you make a living, is it? Your mother would be proud of you!"

Unfortunately, that just egged him on. He growled, raised his club higher, and was about to bring it down on my head—all the time my heart pounding so hard, I thought I might faint—when suddenly I guess he thought better of smashing my head in. Instead he grabbed my hair with his other hand and began to pull me forward.

"Jenny! Jenny!" I cried. But Jenny was nowhere to be seen.

Some of the other girls heard me and tried to get the gorilla off me, but a policeman grabbed them, and soon we were all being pulled toward the paddy wagon. Now not only did I feel faint, but I wanted to be sick. Arrested? I was to be arrested?

I kicked and screamed, but the more I struggled, the more it hurt. He was practically pulling my hair out! And somehow, before I knew it, I was thrown into the wagon. Jenny was already there, along with at least ten other women and girls. The doors closed. The wagon lurched forward.

I sat there in the dark with the other women. No one spoke a word. I was too terrified to even think.

This strike was a serious business—that much I now realized. Police and factory owners were going to do anything to break the will of the strikers— anything. And then I thought of Mama. And I was at least glad that it was me here instead of her.

Or was I?

Chapter 8

I DIDN'T KNOW WHERE WE WERE BEING TAKEN. I HAD BEEN out of the East Side once, when Mama had taken me to Macy's department store. We had walked through the aisles smelling the expensive perfumes, gazing at the hats and scarves; we even tried on a skirt each! But everything Mama showed me was for a purpose.

"You see, Rosie," she had said, "these are the things we make for a few cents an hour. They are sold at a huge profit in these stores to people who are rich because we work for so little. This is not fair, Rosie. This is what I'm working to change."

I peered through the dark of the wagon until I was able to spot Jenny. I crawled over to her. She put her arm around me to help me calm down.

"You must tell them your real age," Jenny whispered. "Pretend you were caught up in the strike by accident."

I knew right away that wasn't possible. I'd be in even more trouble with both the authorities and my parents if they knew I wasn't in school. Or that's what I thought at the time. That was my reasoning. So when the wagon stopped and we were moved into the courthouse and then the jail, I didn't say a word. I went into the cell with the others.

There were about twenty of us strikers in the cell, as well as some other people. We sat on the thin benches and waited. Jenny gave me a look and shook her head at me for not speaking up.

It must have been hours before we were brought before the judge. He spoke English, and most of the girls didn't understand him. We weren't asked anything, just placed before him one by one. He would crash his gavel and pronounce either a fine or a prison term. I don't know how he decided. He didn't seem interested in any of the facts. It was enough for him that we had been picketing. I was confused. Picketing wasn't illegal, was it? I had not seen any of the girls hit anyone or be violent. Yet we were being given sentences?

When it was my turn, the judge asked me my name and age. I told him my name and that I was sixteen.

"You are a young girl," he said, his face turning

red. "Perhaps you do not realize that you are striking against God! Against God and humanity."

"No, Your Honor," I answered honestly, "I did not realize that." Did he truly see the strikers as evil women? That's what it sounded like to me.

His face got redder and he glared at me.

"You are not allowed to speak to the judge," he said. "Fifty-dollar fine!"

"But I don't have any money at all!" I answered.

"Five days in jail, then."

Mama and Papa would be frantic with worry. They would think something dreadful had happened to me.

Suddenly Jenny was beside me. "Your Honor, she's only a child."

"This one talks too? Bailiff! Have both these women removed. I'm not sure five days in jail is sufficient for such impudence. But it will have to do for now."

Under her breath I heard her murmur, *"Ver dershtikt!"* a retort to the judge which she could never have said loud enough to be heard, as it meant, "Choke yourself!" I realized then that Jenny never spoke Yiddish. Like me, she must have decided at some point that it wasn't American enough. At that moment, I liked her even more.

Jenny and I were taken back to the jail. It was then that I truly began to panic. Not on my account, but on Mama's. My unexplained absence was sure to make her ill all over again! What had I been thinking of, not heeding Jenny's advice?

The cell we were in was so filthy, I couldn't imagine how we were to spend five days there. And to make matters worse, a woman was thrown into the cell with us who seemed to take an immediate dislike to me. From the way she was dressed, I could see she was not a striker.

"What are you looking at?" she demanded.

"Nothing," I answered.

She strode over to me and pulled me by the hair. I gasped in pain. *It'll be a miracle if I have a hair left on my head after today,* I thought. I let out a shriek and somehow a giggle, too.

"Something funny?" she asked, pulling harder.

"No!" I gasped.

Her breath stank as she leaned over me and hissed, "Is there something you want to say, then?"

"No," I answered, bewildered at what she thought I might want to say.

"Good. Then keep your fancy trap shut."

Fancy? I thought. I hardly looked like a lady. But compared to her, maybe.

She dropped my hair and went to lean against the bars. "What a bunch of saps," she said, looking at us all. "Do you really think you'll get anywhere with this strike? Oh, yeah, I've heard about it. We all have. You're better off doing like us. Steal from them before they steal from you!"

No one wanted to argue with her; she looked far too tough. None of the women answered. Just then a guard opened the cell door and said, "Everyone brought in from the strike is free to leave. One of those fancy dames from uptown has paid all your bail and fines."

As he spoke, a young woman wearing a stunning blue hat and a blue dress walked up behind him, calling, "Come now, friends. No time to lose. We have far more work to do!"

"This is wonderful." Jenny smiled. "Our sisters from the suffragette movement!"

And so, before I knew it, I was out of jail and given trolley fare by the fine lady to get back home. Jenny went with me, and as we were traveling back home she warned me about being more careful. I couldn't afford to get caught again.

"On the other hand," she mused, "I think it would tear at people's hearts to know what happened to us. Especially with your being so young."

She paused for a moment. "Rosie, I'd like you to consider coming to a meeting with me tomorrow and telling others what you've been through today."

"But I've never done anything like that," I objected. "I might sound foolish."

Jenny laughed. "You aren't saying you are frightened, are you? Because if you aren't afraid to be on the picket line and to confront the gorillas, how afraid could you be of talking?"

I couldn't think of a good answer, so I agreed to do it. Once. Only once.

It was almost dark by the time we got back to our street. I hurried home, hoping Mama had not yet begun to worry.

I walked into the apartment and was greeted by the wonderful aroma of Mama's vegetable soup. She always put a meat bone in it for taste. *She must be much better!* I thought. But I found her in bed, sleeping.

"She had me do the shopping, but she insisted on cooking," Abe explained. "Being on her feet for so long was too much for her."

"She's not sick again, is she?" I asked him.

"I don't think so," he said. "She says she overdid it a bit. Where were you? You should have been doing the cooking!"

"I know," I said apologetically. "I promise, tomorrow I'll be home in time to cook and clean and shop and everything."

Abe eyed Mama's skirt. "Were you in school? I didn't see you there."

"Of course I was," I said.

Joe looked up from his book. "She's lying." Joe always knew when I lied.

"Joe!"

Right at that moment Papa walked in. "Ah, that smells good. Is Mama all right?"

"We think she did too much today, Papa," I said before the boys could get started. "I promise to be home in time tomorrow so she won't."

He looked at me intensely for a moment. "Rosie, this is no time for you to be on the street playing your games. Mama needs you."

"Yes, Papa." I wanted to ask him how the nickelodeons were doing, but he went straight in to see Mama. I was lucky he hadn't noticed I was still wearing Mama's long skirt. I quickly changed out of it and busied myself setting the table.

The next morning I waited anxiously for Papa to leave for work, saw the boys off to school, and brought Mama her tea and a roll in bed. As she ate her breakfast I put on her long skirt and hurried off.

I met Jenny in front of the shop. "I was at strike headquarters most of the night," she said. "We've set up meeting rooms all over. Come along to one. Girls are gathering in these rooms to get their placards and to find out information. Some are deciding whether or not to stick it out. Some have just left their machines and are deciding whether or not to join. We want to have speakers all the time, in all the rooms, to help the girls make the right decision."

We walked over to Allen Street, where the union had rented a room on the fourth floor of a building. It was unheated, and there weren't any chairs in the room. A man was speaking. He was instructing the women—there must have been at least twenty—about how to picket.

"Walk together, in twos. Try not to let anyone break through the line. If someone hits you, try not to hit back, because *you'll* be arrested, they won't. We are trying to have someone at the jail at all times in case you are arrested, but there isn't bail money or fine money for everyone, so you may have to pay to get out, or even stay in jail. Some judges are fining girls just for calling out the word 'scab.' We need to think of a way around that. Any chance you get, try to convince the scabs that they are hurting themselves as well as us."

Jenny put up her arm, and he waved us forward. "We were just in jail," she said. "I thought Rosie could tell her story."

"Yes, good idea," he said. "And after that I'd like to continue with a little history of the trade labor unions."

Jenny pushed me to the front of the room. I drew my sweater around me and tried not to shiver. Faces stared back at me, older women and young girls, all wrapped in shawls or old jackets or sweaters. Some were stamping their feet to keep warm. What to say?

"My mama believes in you all," I began slowly. "She's been working for the union for years. She can't be here because she's sick from too much work. But she won't stop." Somehow thinking about Mama helped me to forget about feeling self-conscious; instead, I wanted to speak for her. "My mama knows that if we all stick together we'll be strong. But if we fight one another, we'll be weak. She'd say that we mustn't give up. She'd say that they'll try everything to get us to give up—even put us in jail. I was hiding from the gorillas like Jenny told me to, but they still threw me in the wagon. And they were going to keep us in jail for five days. But I hadn't done anything! Is that fair?"

To my surprise, everyone yelled, "No!"

"Is that right?"

Again everyone yelled, "No!"

"And the judge, he told me that I was striking against God. But why should God, if he exists, be on the owners' side?" I asked. "Because they are rich? Does that make sense?"

Once more the women yelled, "No!"

"But we are striking for our health. For our very lives. Isn't that true?"

They all screamed, "Yes!" Cheering and clapping filled the room. Jenny was actually smiling. I saw the union man give her a nod of approval.

Jenny came up to me. "You are good at this," she said. "Now let's go to the meeting for our shop. We've found a hall on Hester Street, and that's where our girls are going."

In no time, we were there. The room was similar to the last one: no heat, no chairs. Maria was standing in the crowd. I overheard many of the girls arguing for a return to work, now that the point had been made. Jenny had me get up to speak again. This time, when I mentioned Mama, they all knew her, and after I'd finished speaking, they all agreed to stay out at least one more day.

I was just about to go off to one last meeting before going home when Maria grabbed my sleeve. "I have to tell you something," she said, her voice low.

"What?"

"I'll have to go back to work in a few days if this doesn't end."

"You mean, as a scab?"

She nodded. "I have no choice. We need the money."

"Everyone needs the money," I said. "Our family has no money at all coming in, Maria. We need it more than you."

"Then shouldn't you think about it too?" she suggested.

"Never!" I exclaimed, and then followed Jenny to another meeting. But on the way to the next meeting I wondered if Maria was right. In a matter of days we might have no income at all if Papa's business didn't begin to earn. No food for Mama or the boys. No money for medicine. *This is how they win,* I thought bitterly. *How can anyone hold out when it could mean dying? And what if we starve for months and we still don't win?* I felt so discouraged that I told Jenny I had to get home early to help Mama.

As I passed Mrs. Yoffeh's open door on the landing she called to me. "How much courage have you got?"

"Lots!" I called back defiantly.

But at that moment I felt I had almost none.

Chapter 9

THE NEXT MORNING, I SILL HAD MARIA'S WORDS ON MY MIND. Mama was still very weak. How long could I hold out on strike? Maybe I, too, needed to think about returning to work. I brought Mama her breakfast in bed.

"Mama, you would be so happy to see all the women out on the picket line."

"I want you to tell me everything," Mama said. "Everything you see on your way home from school. And if you can find any newspapers, or if Papa can spare a nickel for one, I would love you to read to me about it."

"Mama," I said, "what do you think of the scabs? Are they bad people?"

"Sit down for a minute," Mama said, "and I'll tell you something."

I sat and helped her sit up in bed against her pillows. I handed her a cup of tea, so she could drink while we talked.

"What makes a person a bad person?" she asked me.

I stopped to think. "I don't know. Maybe they're just bad inside," I suggested.

"Born bad?"

I shrugged.

"When you play your pranks—don't deny it, Rosie—does that make you a bad person?"

"No," I replied.

"Have you done anything lately that you're sorry for?"

I thought a minute. "I feel a little sorry I didn't choose Maria first on my team the other day."

"Does that make you a bad person?"

"No!" I answered again. "But I could perhaps have chosen better—I mean, been a better friend by choosing her first."

"And the scabs," Mama said, "maybe they could make better choices too."

"So they aren't bad, they've just chosen badly?"

Mama smiled. "That's right, Rosie. Now, I *have* met people who are bad, and that's a different story, but most people just make bad choices sometimes. And the scabs, well, they are afraid. They are afraid of letting their families down, of not eating, of being hurt while picketing, of the cold . . . of so much."

"But, Mama, all the women who are striking are afraid of that too."

"Yes, but that's what courage is, *pitzeleh*." Mama called me that as a little joke, since it means "little one," and I'm anything but. "It's doing something even though you are afraid. Some of those women don't need to strike . . . did you know that my young friend Jenny makes twelve dollars a week? And so do I."

"Really?"

"Really. But Lizzy, on the other side of the room, she makes four dollars because she is so slow."

"So Jenny is striking for girls like Lizzy?"

"That's right. And for better conditions for herself. That, too."

She looked at me. "Tell me, why didn't you choose Maria first?"

"Because I wanted to win. Is that wrong?"

"I want us to win this strike," Mama answered.

"But that will help everyone," I said.

"Right you are, Rosie dearest. Winning your game would make you feel very good, but would it help make the world a better place?"

I laughed. "No, Mama."

She smiled back. "But I'm not joking. Now hurry, or you'll be late for school."

"All right, Mama," I said. And I kissed her.

I knew at that moment that I was not going to school and that somehow I had to convince Maria not to be a scab. She would feel badly about it later, I knew she would.

The first thing I saw when I got to the picket line in front of our shop was the scabs running in, Maria with them! When I thought back to the night before, I realized that she had purposefully avoided me, saying she was busy with the children.

As I stood outside I did begin to wonder if I would be able to stand being on the picket line for much longer. It was freezing out! I had on three sweaters *and* Mama's gloves *and* her coat. Other girls weren't so well dressed, and one by one, they had to leave the line to go to the hospital because of frostbite. A bit later in the morning a woman fainted. Just dropped, right there in the street. After the poor woman had been helped up and taken into a meeting room, Jenny told me that we were bound to see more and more of such things, as people were already weak from hunger. Many women were not being paid by the bosses for their last week's work.

Suddenly a young girl swathed in scarves and

sweaters came running down the street yelling, "Greenberger has settled!"

Everyone on the picket line cheered.

"What does that mean?" I asked Jenny, shouting above the din.

"Greenberger owns a small shop, and the girls there all went out on strike when we did. And now he's come to an agreement with his workers."

"But that's wonderful!" I exclaimed.

"It is," she said. "I suspect that many of the owners of the smaller shops will settle. They can't afford to miss working days any more than the workers can. It's the large shops like the Triangle factory that will be hard to break."

After a quick lunch Jenny and I went to a meeting on Delancey Street. There were some suffragettes there, and one of them spoke. She pointed out that when men went on strike, they were not jailed or fined. Rarely, at least. She also reminded us why we were receiving such harsh treatment.

"Until women have the vote," she said, "we will never have any power, and men will treat us as they please. Even the union bosses—did they want this strike? No. Even they don't take us seriously."

It was a rousing speech and seemed to pick up everyone's spirits.

After the meeting Jenny and I hurried along Hester Street, heading back to our own shop. As we arrived, we ran into a group of girls who were about to enter Berger's. It was clear that they intended to resume work. I spotted Maria among them, and suddenly got so angry. They were earning money and working, while we were eating potatoes for dinner every night now. Soon we wouldn't even be able to afford a penny herring! I wanted to call out, *Scabs!* But I knew if I did, I'd be arrested. There were police and gorillas everywhere. But if the girls couldn't be shamed into not being scabs, what would stop them? So I yelled, "Strike! Strike! There's a strike at Berger's. Strike!"

Jenny gave me a look that was worth a piece of strudel. "Good thinking," she said, and she took up the chant. "Strike, strike, there's a strike at Berger's."

Soon people from the street began to gather. Lots of people. The scabs were trapped and couldn't get through the crowd. Within a quarter hour there must have been a thousand people in the street and they started chanting, "Scabs, scabs!" Well, the police couldn't arrest all of them and besides, those who weren't on strike could say what they liked.

The police had to form a corridor to allow the scabs to pass through the crowd. Some of the girls made it into the building, running, caught in the crowd. I saw Maria and I did feel a twinge of conscience when I saw the look of fear in her eyes, but why was she persisting with this? Did she want *me* to starve? I was starting to take this personally. And it *was* personal, wasn't it?

The rest of the scabs were trying to get inside. The crowd began to jostle them, attempting to break through the police line. In response, the police lifted their arms and began to bring down their clubs on the strikers.

Maria was only a few feet away. Then I heard her scream. She was in danger of being trampled by the surging crowd. I ducked under the police line, leaped into the crowd of scabs and threw myself in front of her, saying, "Stay close, I'll protect you!"

But a policeman saw me breach the line. "Get out of here, you troublemaker!" he yelled at me. He then reached over, grabbed me by my coat, and dragged me off. I tried to struggle, knowing that if I came before the judge again, I'd be in terrible trouble.

Suddenly Maria shouted at the policeman. "Let her go! Let her go! She's one of us! Couldn't you see, she was trying to help me?"

I was shocked. Maria never stood up to anyone!

"I'm sure I saw this one on the other side!" he protested.

"No, no, she's with us. Let her go."

Reluctantly, he loosened his grip on me. I grabbed Maria's hand and the two of us ducked under arms, squeezed past a shouting line of strikers and scabs, and pushed past other groups of picketers until we were finally away from the crush of people.

We stood panting, hearts pounding, still gripping each other's hands.

Finally Maria said, "Rosie, you're going to crush every finger I have left."

"What do you mean, 'left'?" I asked.

"I don't know," she replied. And then she burst out laughing. And so did I. It seemed like the funniest thing I'd ever heard. I started laughing and couldn't stop! So did Maria. We stood in the street, people hurrying past us, laughing until tears welled in our eyes. We put our arms around each other and our hands on each other's shoulders and laughed more. I got the hiccups. And that made us laugh even harder. We sank against a building for support because we were so weak with laughter that, otherwise, we would have ended up on the ground.

Finally, exhausted, Maria took my hand and we began to walk home.

"Why did you do it?" she asked.

"What?"

"Protect me?"

I put my arm around her waist. "Because you're my friend. . . . Why'd you do it?" I asked.

"What?"

"Protect me?"

"Because you're my friend," she replied.

We walked in silence for a while. "Papa says he doesn't believe in God," I began.

"I know," she answered.

"But he told me that we should do to others what we'd want done to us. He says he's learned some good things from being Jewish." I paused. "The thing is, I know you need the money, Maria. But if everyone doesn't strike together, we'll never get the owners to agree to our demands."

Maria started to speak. "But—," she began.

"No, wait. Don't argue yet. I know your papa wants you to work. But he knows how sick Mama is. And she's sick because of how hard the work is. You'll get sick too, if things don't improve. I'll be fine. I'll go back to school. But you have to think ahead. Let me talk to your father. Please."

Maria was silent for a moment. "All right. Come now and talk to him. If you can convince him, then I promise I'll join you."

I had to think fast on the way home. By the time we arrived, I still wasn't sure what I was going to say to Mr. Vaccaro. Maria's father worked in a shoe factory. Perhaps he'd understand, then?

When we got to Maria's apartment, dinner was already finished. Mr. Vaccaro was getting the table ready for his friends to come over and play cards.

"Poppy," Maria said, "can Rosie talk to you?"

"Of course," he said. He was a strict man, and I was a little afraid of him. Yet he always seemed to treat his children fairly.

"Sit," he offered.

I sat. I knew his English wasn't very good, so I had to choose my words carefully. "Mr. Vaccaro," I began, "this strike is very dangerous. Maria was almost very badly hurt today."

"Rosie saved me!" Maria interrupted.

"Well, Maria returned the favor," I said. "But it is bad right now, with big fights. Maybe she should go back to school until it's all over," I said quickly, not being able to think of anything better.

"Are you at school?" he asked.

I paused. "Yes."

"Then you two go together, every morning, and she will not go against the strike," he agreed.

And that was the end of the interview. We huddled in the front room in the corner, away from the others.

Maria looked disappointed.

"Aren't you happy?" I whispered. "You can go back to school. You don't have to fight us anymore."

"I *am* happy," she said. "I hated doing that."

"Why don't you look happy, then?" I asked.

"I'm worried about you."

"Me? Why?"

"You lied to my father."

"I had to!"

"And you've been lying to your mama and papa."

"But I'm doing some good. And they wouldn't let me if they knew."

"So in order to do good, it means you can be bad—and lie?"

"That's not fair!"

"Isn't it? Aren't you trying to make people's lives better?"

"Yes!"

"And are you doing that by lying to the ones closest to you?"

"It's not like that!"

Maria gave me a knowing look. "You have to think about this," she said.

I stared at her. "I suppose I do," I said reluctantly.

On my way back to my apartment Mrs. Yoffeh called to me from across the landing. "Big changes coming!"

I was sick of this. I stalked over to her and stood at her door. "How do you know all this, Mrs. Yoffeh?" I demanded.

"I just do," she answered simply. She was a small, plump woman, with gray hair and gray eyes. Her clothes were always unusual. She was wearing a purple skirt and a yellow shirtwaist. Her front room was covered in prints and doilies and lacework everywhere. It all looked rather festive and pretty, I had to admit.

"You seem to shout things to me, although not out loud," she said with a smile. "I have people who come here all the time, and often I see nothing for them. You walk by and I see everything! It's just like that sometimes. I can't explain it." She paused. "I'm glad your mama is better."

I softened a little inside. "Do you think the praying helped?"

"I think so," she said. "After all, how could I see

the future if there wasn't a future to see? God's hand must be there."

"Mama says the opposite."

"Just remember," she said to me, "the future is the decisions we make today."

Had she overheard me and Maria?

"Don't look at me like that." She laughed, her funny sort of cackle. "You don't have to be psychic to read the look on your face. You have some choices to make."

"Hard choices," I agreed.

Suddenly Abe was racing past me from the Vaccaroses' apartment to ours. I turned to follow him, knowing he would tease me for talking to Mrs. Yoffeh.

And I couldn't help but wonder, *What big changes?*

Chapter 10

"ROSIE," MAMA ANNOUNCED WHEN I WALKED INTO OUR apartment. "I feel ready to go out."

"Mama!" I said. "Papa won't allow it. The doctor said two weeks."

"But," she complained, "I feel so much better!"

I noticed that she had already started dinner. "Mama, you will overdo it," I said. "If you are more patient, you'll get better faster," I pleaded. I thought to myself, *And you won't find out so soon what I've been up to.*

I made her sit down. "Mama, I'm going to finish dinner and I'm going to clean up, and you are to sit and read the newspaper." I noticed Abe had brought her one.

While I did that, I thought about what to do. Mama was getting better. One day soon I'd be giving a talk or picketing, and Mama would show up. This didn't seem so unlikely anymore. At any rate, she was bound to find out where I'd been and what I'd been doing.

As I skinned the potatoes my stomach grumbled as I thought of the days when we could eat chicken once a week, and the days when Mama gave the boys and me a penny for candy every day. Now I was preparing potatoes and nothing else. Perhaps Mama assumed that was because her wage wasn't coming in, but she would no doubt begin asking Papa why *he* had no wage and why we were eating so poorly.

Just as I was thinking this, Papa came home— and in his hands, a chicken. An entire chicken!

"Drop that in your boiling water, Rosie." Papa grinned. From his other hand, with a flourish, he produced a bag full of carrots and onions. "And throw these in as well!"

The boys crowded around him, and he lavished hugs and kisses on them, and then on Mama, too.

"We're making a profit already," he said. "This will change everything!"

"A profit?" Mama asked. "At the theater?"

"Come, Celia," he said. "I have something to tell you."

He and Mama went into the back room. I

assumed he was about to *finally* tell her about the nickelodeons.

By the time I'd finished preparing the dinner, it was late. Mama and Papa had been in the back room talking the entire time. Joe had his nose in a book, and Abe was doing his homework. I removed the oilcloth from the table and laid out our white lace cloth. I made sure all the dishes were spotless, and then I called everyone to eat.

First we had the broth. After that I served the boiled chicken and the vegetables. Mama was quiet as Papa chattered on about what a wonderful new beginning the new business would be.

I'd been to a nickelodeon, of course, with Mama and the boys. We sat through the picture three times, as it was only a half hour in length. We'd had to stand in line for ages, but while waiting, everyone talked and laughed, ate pretzels and apples, and had a wonderful time. I just wished we'd had the time to go again. Mama had taken us only that once, because she was always busy with her union work. As soon as I thought about the union, I once again realized that my secret was bound to come out soon. Before I could think about it anymore and change my mind, I blurted out the truth.

"I haven't been going to school," I said quietly,

cutting Papa off in the middle of a sentence.

There was a dead silence as everyone stared at me.

Papa's eyes narrowed. "Where have you been going, Rosie?"

"I've been out on the picket lines."

Again dead silence.

Mama looked furious. She opened her mouth to say something when Papa burst out laughing.

"This is hardly the time for that," Mama reprimanded him.

Joe shook his head at me. "I knew you were lying."

"*Shah!*" I hissed at him.

Papa's face became more serious. He looked at Mama. "You can hardly be surprised," he said. "You've done nothing but teach her about the need for a union for years. Well, now she's following what you taught her."

"I don't understand," Mama said. "How did you get involved with the union in the first place?"

"When you were sick, Mama," I said, "I went to work in your place."

Mama stood up, her cheeks turning red. "You did what?"

"I went to work. I had to, Mama. We needed the

money. Not," I added, "that I've actually been paid. The strike started right after I began at the shop."

"You knew this?" she said, turning to Papa.

"I knew she was working," he admitted. "We were in a spot, Celia. I'd just given all my savings for the nickelodeons."

"Which," Mama interrupted, "I didn't find out about until just now! I obviously cannot afford to fall sick again. I'll wake up, and we'll be in Timbuktu, with Papa chief of the local village and Rosie organizing their union!" She looked at Abe. "Have you anything to admit to?"

"No!" he said. "Well," he added, "no more than usual."

Mama looked at Joe. "I'm not so sure about even you," she said. "Perhaps you're a spy in your spare time."

I laughed, despite all the trouble I was in.

"It's true what Papa says, Rosie," Mama said, sitting back down. "I can't say I haven't taught you well. On the one hand, I'm glad in a way that you had the courage to stick it out with the others. On the other hand, I'm very unhappy with you."

"Lying," Papa explained, "can never be excused."

"But I had to," I exclaimed. "You would never have let me. And I had to help with the strike. I didn't want Mama to go back to work there again. I found out for myself how horrible working in that shop is. She would surely just get sick all over again."

Papa's face was grim. "What did I just say, Rosie?"

"You said lying can never be excused."

"And what did you just do?"

"I made an excuse," I admitted. "But *never*, Papa? Didn't you tell me not to tell Mama?"

"She has a point," Abe agreed.

Papa grimaced and looked at Mama. She shook her head at him.

"We just didn't *tell* Mama," he said. "That's different."

"How?" I asked.

"How, indeed?" Mama said. "I understand your papa didn't want to worry me when I was sick, and perhaps that was wrong, but it was a judgment he made because of my health. In your case, you have no such excuse. You have an important lesson to learn, Rosie. You must do the right thing because it is right—and not worry what the consequences will be. You tell the truth because it is the right thing. Maybe Papa would have said yes to your being on the picket line, maybe he would have said no. But that was not for you to decide. You made a bad choice, Rosie, even though your intentions were good. Even though you thought you were lying for a good reason."

"Plus, it's dangerous out there," Papa added. "People are being arrested."

Something in my face then must have given me away.

"Rosie! No!"

"It wasn't so bad, Papa. And the union lady paid my fine."

"What was it like?" Abe wanted to know, eyes shining. "I can say my sister's been in the clink!"

"You should have trusted me, Rosie. Isn't that what we do as a family? Count on one another?" Papa said. He looked sad.

I felt crushed. I'd expected them to be angry, but deep down I thought they'd be pleased. I didn't think they would be disappointed in me. I finished my food in silence. Joe took over the conversation, telling Mama all about the new book he was reading. When dinner was over, Mama went to bed, all tired out.

Papa called me over to the couch. "Tell me what you've been doing this past week, Rosie."

So I told him everything that had happened.

When I was finished, he said, "All right. I'm tempted to force you to go back to school, but I don't want you to see school as a punishment for bad behavior. You've always loved school. So I'll let you stay out until after the holidays. If you stay close to Mama's friend Jenny and promise not to get arrested again, I'll let you continue. You seem to be their good luck charm. But if the strike goes beyond New Year's, you *will* return to school."

"Thank you, Papa," I exclaimed, throwing my arms around him. "I'm very sorry I lied!"

And that was the truth. I *was* sorry. I should have trusted him.

The next morning I was able to leave the house wearing Mama's skirt without having to sneak out—of course, not before she scolded me about lying about that, too. When I got to the shop, the girls were not picketing out in front. I wondered if that was because it was Saturday, but I hurried to the meeting room on Allen Street just in case they were there. I did find most of the girls there, although not all of them. Some of them were probably at home observing Shabbat. Before the strike they had been forced to work on Saturdays or lose their jobs, but no one would force them to attend meetings on a Saturday.

I noticed a man at the front of the room who I'd seen before on the picket lines. His name was Mr. Mulberry. He was a union leader. Jenny was standing at the front of the room with him, and they were having a heated discussion. After listening for a while I realized that the owner, Mr. Berger, must have made an offer and that the strikers were debating whether or not to take it.

"Let me go over the deal with my girls again," Jenny said to Mr. Mulberry. She then turned toward the other girls in the room. "They are offering us a fifty-two hour workweek. No more fines for talking or stretching or singing or bathroom breaks."

"But what about locking us in?" one girl asked.

"What about the overcrowding?" another asked.

"This is a good deal. A fair deal. I'd advise taking it," Mr. Mulberry said.

"What about recognizing the union?" I asked from the back.

"No," he said. "No union recognition."

The girls started to argue among themselves. Finally Jenny said, "I think we should say no, unless they recognize the union. Otherwise, they could fine all of us who have joined."

"I second that," I shouted. Everyone laughed. But when a vote was taken, the offer was defeated.

We huddled in the cold room, talking, trying to keep our spirits up while we waited for Jenny. She had taken our decision back to Mr. Berger.

A few miserable, cold hours later Jenny burst into the room, cheeks pink from running. "They will recognize the union!" she cried. The girls cheered. Some began to weep. Everyone hugged one another.

I wondered about the other demands we had made, but I felt happy, too. Jenny pulled me to the front of the room, and the girls lifted me once again on their shoulders.

"We will continue to work for the girls in other shops, won't we?" Jenny called out.

"Yes!" the others replied.

I ran home as fast as I could to tell Mama the news. To my surprise, I found Papa there, although it was well after his lunch hour. He and Mama were deep in conversation, and they seemed surprised to see me.

"Mama, Mr. Berger has settled!" I exclaimed. "The strike is over at your shop!"

Tears filled Mama's eyes. "That's wonderful news, Rosie! But it's not over for many others, true?"

"True, Mama."

"There is still lots of work to do."

"But Mama won't be doing it here," Papa said. "Rosie, sit."

I sat on the chair. I was getting a funny feeling in the pit of my stomach.

"Rosie, the business is doing so well that Mr. Jacobson and I are going to expand. Mr. Jacobson will stay here—he has to, because of his theater. But we . . . well, Rosie, we are setting off on a real adventure! We are going to Chicago."

"Chicago?"

"Yes, Rosie. You know where that is, don't you?"

"I know it's very far away."

"We'll take a train there. And we'll open up four more nickelodeons!"

For a moment I couldn't speak. "But my friends, Papa."

"You'll make new friends, Rosie. Come on. You are the brave one. It's the boys who will find the change hardest. I depend on you to help."

I thought about that. I *was* pretty brave, wasn't I? If a gorilla couldn't scare me, why should a new city? I threw back my shoulders. "All right, Papa. You can depend on me."

Papa smiled. "I knew I could. We won't leave until Mama is stronger. We'll be here for the holidays."

I couldn't wait for Maria to get home from school. When she finally did, I caught her in the hallway. Before I could tell Maria the news, I noticed Mrs. Yoffeh sitting in her usual spot. She was looking right at me, a small smile on her face.

"Big changes, Rosie?" Mrs. Yoffeh called.

"Yes," I called back. "You were right again."

She cackled. "You finally admit it?"

"I admit it."

I grabbed Maria and pulled her into our apartment and told her what was going on. She was very sad. But we promised we would write to each other all the time.

"Papa says I am brave," I said to her, "but suddenly I don't feel all that brave. What if I can't make new friends? I know everyone around here. It'll feel so lonely there!"

"Only at first," she said. "You *will* make friends," she assured me.

"And it *will* be exciting." I grinned. "Going on a train! And so far away. Anything could happen."

Maria smiled. "Everything is an adventure to you, Rosie!"

It was my final game of ring-a-levio. I was awarded the title of captain, since it was my last game on

Orchard Street. This time I had no trouble deciding whom I'd choose first: Maria. We won the toss,
so we had to hide. I crept behind a pushcart, pretending to be shopping, as I remembered Martha
had. What a time I'd had the past few weeks! I'd
been on a march to city hall to protest the police
beatings; I'd been to a huge meeting where I got to
sit on the stage with all the others who'd been
jailed. Most of the women had been much worse
off than me. A number of them had been sen-
tenced to the workhouse! They told of dreadful
conditions, and I was relieved that I, at least, was
spared that.

Chicago. *What lies ahead?* I wondered. Then I
couldn't help but giggle. I needn't wonder—I should
just ask Mrs. Yoffeh!

Suddenly arms were around me.

"Gotcha, gotcha, gotcha!"

It was Abe. I easily wriggled out of his grasp and
made a dash for another hiding place. It was the last
game, and I wanted my team to win! And yet I knew
that it was just a game. Somehow I had a different
perspective on things now. I knew that playing with
my friends, and sticking together, was more important than winning. I knew that I was lucky to have
friends and to be able to have fun.

I felt badly for the women still on the picket lines. I hoped they would win their fight. And I would always try to be as brave as they were in everything I did. If I could do this, then I knew I'd be someone Papa and Mama could be proud of.

The most amazing thing about the shirtwaist makers' strike that took place in New York City from the fall of 1909 through the winter of 1910 was that it was mainly young girls—teenagers—who took part. These young girls were instrumental in growing the labor movement into a serious force in the United States. They were incredibly brave, standing up to terrible brutality, fighting for rights we all take for granted now.

Children of Rosie's age regularly worked in the "shops," as the factories were called, mainly as snippers. They could not afford to go to school, as their families needed their wages. By the age of fourteen most young people were out of school and working.

Unfortunately, Rosie's fear about a fire breaking out in a locked factory did come true. There was a dreadful fire a year after the shirtwaist makers' strike, in March 1911. It began on the eighth floor of the Triangle Shirtwaist Factory. Because the men who had negotiated the end of the strike thought working conditions were less important than wages, they allowed owners to continue the practice of locking in their workers. When the fire raced through the factory, the locked doors doomed the poor girls. One hundred forty-six people died, some burning to death, others choosing to jump, hand in hand, to their deaths. After the Triangle factory fire there was a complete overhaul of working conditions. Then things really began to look up for factory workers.

To find out more about this period in history, visit:
http://www.tenement.org/ and
http://womhist.binghamton.edu/shirt/doclist.htm